Is Anybody Listening?

Larry O'Loughlin is a storyteller and author of five books for younger children; he is also co-author of *Our House*, a non-fiction book for adults. One of his titles for younger children, *The Gobán Saor*, illustrated by John Leonard, was shortlisted for the 1997 Bisto Book of the Year Award. *Is Anybody Listening?* is his first book for teenagers. Larry lives in Dublin with his wife and family. He is the father of award-winning teenage author Aislinn O'Loughlin.

For Monica, for caring so much through so many lives

'In their little worlds in which children have their existence,
there is nothing so finely perceived and so finely felt
as injustice ....'

Charles Dickens, *Great Expectations*

Is Anybody Listening?

Larry O'Loughlin

WOLFHOUND PRESS

First published in 1999 by
Wolfhound Press Ltd
68 Mountjoy Square
Dublin 1, Ireland
Tel: (353-1) 874 0354
Fax: (353-1) 872 0207

A percentage of the author's royalties from the sale of this book will go to Mukti Ashram.

This book is fiction. All characters, incidents and names have no connection with any persons living or dead. Any apparent resemblance is purely coincidental.

 Wolfhound Press receives financial assistance from The Arts Council/An Chomhairle Ealaíon, Dublin, Ireland.

British Library Cataloguing in Publication Data
A catalogue record for this book is available from the British Library.

ISBN 0-86327-721-7

10 9 8 7 6 5 4 3 2 1

'Whatever You Want' — words and music by Rick Parfitt and Andy Bown. Reproduced by kind permission of EMI Music Publishing Ltd, London WC2H 0EA, England.
'Rockin' All Over the World' — words and music by John Fogerty. Reproduced by kind permission of John Fogerty/Wenaha Music Company.
'Jack Daniels' and 'The Dublin Two-Step' — words and music by Niall Toner. Reproduced by kind permission of Bardis Music.
'Paradise Drive OK' — words and music by Larry O'Loughlin. Reproduced by kind permission of Velvet Music.

Cover illustration: The Slide File
Cover Design: Slick Fish Design, Dublin
Typesetting: Wolfhound Press
Printed and bound by The Guernsey Press Co., Guernsey, Channel Islands

prologue

The girl can feel the dark.

It has been there all morning.

At first, it was hardly noticeable — just two pencil-thin grey lines resting somewhere at her temples.

But now it has grown.

Now it forms two thick black wedges that press hard on the edges of *that* place, her secret place, where the voices come and the pictures dance.

Soon the dark will close.

Like the shutter of a camera, it will close over the last remaining light in *that* place, surrounding it with its thick, solid blackness.

And then?

The 'And then?' frightens the girl. It makes her pulse race and her heart beat faster. It makes tiny beads of perspiration trickle down the back of her neck and stick her long hair to her skin.

And so she fights. She fights with all her will, trying desperately to hold back the encroaching dark.

~

The girl's name is Laura Byrne. She is seventeen. She is tall and slightly chubby. She has sallow skin, curly dark hair and dark brown eyes. She is attractive and bright, and she is frightened. She is very, very frightened.

From somewhere outside herself, she hears a harsh, almost hysterical voice.

'You're wrong!'

Laura knows that voice. She has heard it before, somewhere.

Oh Christ!

It's her! Some part of her that is not fighting the dark has spoken, hurling out the words like stones fired from a slingshot.

Laura Byrne wouldn't do that. She wouldn't sound so angry and aggressive, not to Miss O'Toole. She would be polite. She would say, 'Sorry, Miss, that's not true,' and her voice would be soft and respectful. But it isn't her. It is the dark, and the dark has no respect. The dark is squeezing the breath out of her, forcing her into two, three, many Laura Byrnes, and it is one of those Laura Byrnes that has screeched.

She looks up. Miss O'Toole sits still, made motionless by the sound. One hand is frozen behind her head, where it had been playing with the long, thin pigtail that hangs from the back of her tightly cut hair. Her young face is flushed. Behind the large red-framed glasses, Miss O'Toole's soft blue eyes are wide with surprise.

Laura feels every face in the class is turning to her. They are watching, waiting to see what she'll do next. She has their complete attention. She can do what she wants with them, take them anywhere. But she doesn't want them.

She looks towards the teacher, pleading, raising her hand and shaking her head in a wordless apology. The teacher nods her acceptance.

'So, Laura.' Miss O'Toole smiles, taking back the class. 'You disagree with what I said?'

'I .... Yes, Miss .... Well, it's just that ....'

The words do not come. Images whirl around her mind. If she can only hold one long enough to give it a name, she will answer.

Her throat is tightening. She feels sick. Her forehead and cheeks begin to burn.

'Take your time, Laura. It's obviously something you feel strongly about.'

Is it? She doesn't know. The Laura Byrne who doesn't fight the dark has a point to make, but what is it?

She takes a deep breath. From somewhere, the words and ideas come.

'It's just — you're wrong when you say it like that, Miss. It's not like that. Not for everyone. I mean, I know you're right: sniffing glue or solvents can kill people. There was that little girl with the Tipp-Ex a few years ago, and when we were in second year there was Brian Feely —'

'What a prat he was!' a voice behind Laura whispers.

Miss O'Toole is angry. 'Conor Meade, if that's the extent of your contribution to the class, maybe you'd like to stay behind after school and learn a little more about the subject. Would you?'

'No, Miss. Sorry, Miss.'

'Right, then keep quiet and let Laura carry on. Laura?'

Laura closes her eyes tightly. The interruption has thrown her. She is frantically trying to remember what she was saying.

'It's just ... it's just ....'

What is happening to me?

The dark is fluttering and swirling and dissolving. It is moving, black to grey to white to black to blacker ....

Now, in that place where the voices come and the pictures dance, there is no more than a finger's width that is not given up to the dark.

Laura takes another deep breath, letting the words come slowly, thinking only of one word at a time.

'It's not right to say everyone does it for the buzz. If you're really poor and living on the streets or sleeping in railway stations, like all those thousands of kids in the old communist countries, then for a few seconds it's a way to escape the cold and the hunger and the poverty and ....'

Images are swimming through that tiny gap left between the swirling wedges of the dark. They frighten her, yet they reassure her. She knows the images. They are old friends. She has been to those places, done those things, known those people, that girl whose name is ... whose name is ....

What is her name?

Rosa!

Laura's voice is beginning to rise. Tears are welling up in her eyes. She can't carry on.

'You're right, of course.' Miss O'Toole smiles at her gently. 'What I said earlier was a generalisation. I was talking about this country, and particularly this area. But even those poor kids you've just mentioned are still at risk, you'll agree?'

Laura nods. It is all she can do.

'So, whether you do it for the buzz or out of a sense of complete hopelessness, like those kids, you can still die — first, fifth or fifty-first time. No one ever knows. It's like Russian roulette.' Miss O'Toole places two fingers against her temple and brings her thumb down against them, imitating the action of the hammer of a pistol. 'You're always gambling with death.'

Laura knows about death.

'And now, my dear fifth-years, I'd like ....' The buzzer for the end of the period rings, cutting Miss O'Toole's words short. 'OK, don't rush down the corridors. See you soon.'

Laura waits. When the others are out of the room, she will force herself out of her chair. She listens to the babble in the corridors. The noise is deafening. For years she has been one of the first out of the room, heading down the corridor with Sarah and Cass and Tina, but now she waits alone.

She pulls her sports bag onto her shoulder, stands up and pushes the chair under the desk with her knees.

A voice whispers in her ear.

'You OK?'

She looks up. It's Declan Donnelly. The class quiet man, the one who disappeared for a year — no one knows where — and came back changed, quieter. He's looking at her quizzically.

Laura nods, and he walks off.

Miss O'Toole waits at the door.

Laura rummages inside her sports bag. She pretends she's looking for something.

Please, Miss, go away, she pleads silently. *Just go away and leave me alone.*

'Well, Laura, how's it going?'

'Fine, Miss, fine.' Laura doesn't look up. 'Just making sure I have my wristband .... Oh, there it is.'

She zips the bag again, slings it over her shoulder and walks quickly to the door, looking at the ground.

Miss O'Toole stands between her and the corridor. 'You're sure it's fine? You didn't seem to be your old self today, or last week.'

'No, I'm fine, honest,' Laura lies. 'It's just that I ... I

still haven't really got over that asthma attack last week. I'm still a bit wheezy and it's hard to sleep.'

'Yeah, it can be a real bitch.' Miss O'Toole's reply is unconvincing.

Laura looks at the teacher. The urge to tell her is almost too great. But she doesn't tell. There is no one she can tell who will understand.

'Laura, you know where I am if you need to talk.'

Laura nods.

'Well, you'd better head along, then.'

As Laura steps past, Miss O'Toole glances down at the sleeves of her red school blazer.

Christ! She doesn't believe me. She's checking for glue stains. She'll be checking my locker next, for aerosols.

Head down, Laura counts the black and white tiles on the floor as she walks to the changing room.

If I concentrate on counting, the pictures and the dark will go, she tells herself, hoping. *Fifty-seven, fifty-eight, fifty-nine ....*

Hands grab her roughly and pin her against the lockers with a thud.

'What the hell do you think you're doing?' Conor demands. His face is flushed with anger.

'Take your hands off me before my knee turns you into a soprano,' Laura hisses, kicking out at him.

Conor's grip loosens, but he doesn't move away. She still can't move.

'Come on, Laura, what are you doing?'

Laura glares at him. He has long fair hair tied back in a ponytail. The start of a moustache is beginning to sprout on his upper lip. Some people might think he's attractive — he certainly does — but Laura knows him too well. They've been in the same class since playschool, and they've been mixed-doubles badminton partners since they started secondary school.

'Conor, get out of my way or I'll break your neck.'

'I'm not moving till you tell me what you're at. I've seen you talking to Gnasher and the other scummers, but I thought you were just doing your "Hey, I'm a socialist, I talk to anyone" bit. But after what you said in class .... It explains a lot about why you've been like this the last few weeks. For God's sake, Laura, you don't need that stuff.'

'What stuff?' Laura replies angrily. She pushes him away. 'You don't know anything.'

Conor grabs her by the arm and spins her around. 'You know what I'm talking about. Christ! If you want to try that sort of crap, ask me. I can get you some really good blow from my friends at university. You don't have to —'

Laura shakes her arm free and glares at him.

'Conor, you're such a dickhead. You hang around the university badminton club with your brother, drinking Jack Daniels and smoking dope, and you think you're so cool. Well, you're not. You're an idiot. You think you're better than Gnasher's crowd? Don't fool yourself! You've no idea what I'm on about, but believe me, I'm no prat!'

She storms towards the girls' changing-room. Conor grabs the handle of her sports bag.

'Laura, you know what you mean to me. I don't want to see you doing anything ....'

Laura barges into the changing-room. Conor follows her. He is still holding on to her bag.

'It's just that —'

'Conor! *Get lost*!' Laura screams at him.

'Yeah, Conor, get lost!' the other girls in the changing-room yell. Conor is hit with a barrage of sport shoes and socks.

'You bitch,' a voice giggles behind Laura, not really

meaning it. A bra, red lace with black frilly edges, lands on Conor's shoulder. Laura recognises the bra. She sniffs derisively.

Conor smiles. He tucks the bra into his inside pocket.

'I'll keep this as a souvenir. So nice to see all of you, ladies.'

~

Laura is only slightly aware of the sounds and movements around her; only slightly aware that she is changing from her uniform into her badminton clothes; only gradually aware that she is alone.

She walks to the gym door. She pushes the door open and steps onto the badminton court.

Suddenly, she feels that she is burning up from the inside out. Her chest tightens. For a second the dark takes complete control. It swirls around her, its black-grey-whiteness pouring into her ears and up her nose, burning her eyes and clogging her mouth and throat, choking her. She can feel the dark. She can taste it. She can hear it crackling and hissing around her.

Then she can see again. The darkness clings to her mouth and throat, forcing her to gasp for every breath. The taste of the dark makes her stomach heave. She feels dizzy and sick, but she can see again. The dark has lifted from her eyes.

And in *that* place, her secret place, there is a light. It is no wider than a fingernail, but it is light.

Laura throws her racket down at the side of the court and walks to the changing-room.

'Laura! Laura Byrne!' voices are calling behind her. 'Come back here at ....'

She doesn't stop to change. She grabs her clothes from the peg and sweeps them into her sports bag, all in one movement. She walks down the corridor and out of the school. Voices call her name, faces stare at her, but she keeps walking.

As she stumbles into the house, a voice calls to her from the kitchen. 'Who's that?' It is Chris's voice, her mother's voice. She isn't working in the refuge today.

'Just me. I just came home to get ....' Laura forces herself to reply.

'OK, love,' her mother calls. 'I'll get you a glass of orange for when you're ready to go back.'

Laura struggles up the stairs. Her whole body is soaked in perspiration. Each step takes a supreme effort of will. She can hardly breathe. The darkness is almost total.

She kicks open the door to the bedroom she shares with her eight-year-old sister, Katie. She drops her bag on the floor and flops onto her bed. The burning in her throat, her stomach, her head, is almost unbearable. She puts her hand under her pillow, grabs her diary and flicks it open. She can hardly see it. It is like looking through a dense fog.

Laura lifts her pencil. Her hand shakes so much that she can hardly keep it still as she adds to the words already on the page.

When she is finished she lets the pencil drop and squints at the page. The fog is thicker, and the pictures are whirling around so fast that she can hardly concentrate. The handwriting is a weak scrawl, but she can make out the words she has written:

Today I die. God help me.

She holds the diary to her breast and waits.

~

Laura Byrne has been dying for a long time: days;
weeks. Inch by inch, minute by minute, she has been
slipping away. She knows that now.

And as she waits to die, a small frightened voice
forces itself through the darkness and calls to her.

'Laura, I'm scared,' says the voice.

'Sanjid,' Laura whispers. 'Sanjid.'

~

Somewhere outside there are sounds. The doorbell
ringing, Chris's footsteps down the hall. Hurried,
whispered conversation. Chris calling Laura, calling
her. Footsteps on the stairs, her door being opened. Her
mother shaking her, screaming her name.

More footsteps. Her diary is pulled from her grip.
There is a pounding on her chest, someone forcing her
mouth open and breathing into it. More cries and
screams. There is the sound of an ambulance. Hands
lift her onto something. She is being carried. She wants
to tell them about the blackness, the burning, the
crushing pain in her chest, but she can't. She can't
escape the dark.

'Laura, Laura!' the little voice calls again. 'Laura, it's
Sanjid. I'm scared. There's smoke, burning — I can't
breathe! Help me! Help ....'

The voice inside Laura's head is weak. It is as weak
as she is, and even more frightened.

'Don't worry. I'm with you,' she replies soundlessly,
through the dark. 'I'm with you.'

~

Laura feels the bumping, hears the screaming of the
siren. She hears doors being flung open and feels herself being lifted. Voices are talking quickly, anxiously.
Hands are touching her, prodding her. She hears the

words 'drugs' and 'asthma' and wants to scream, 'No. No! You don't understand!' But she can't scream.

And all the time the voice in her head, Sanjid's voice, is calling weakly, 'Help me. Someone please help me.'

Laura repeats the words. 'Help me. Someone please help me.'

But her words do not penetrate the dark.

Then, through all the words and noise and clatter beyond the darkness, she hears her mother say one word. 'Diary.'

~

Chris Byrne reads the diary. She reads of a life that none of them shared in; an unknown, secret life that her daughter lived beyond the family, beyond friends, beyond the bounds of the body.

~

Laura is floating above the walls, above the room where the doctor and nurses are busy around her body and her mother and teacher sit anxiously. Laura feels no fear as she floats. She likes the feeling.

She watches her mother flicking through her diary, studying each entry. Laura knows those entries, the record of her secret life. As Chris reads, Laura sees each entry relived, as if she is watching a film of her story. She hears the actors speaking their lines, the narrator filling in the details.

And as the opening credits roll, Laura sees that night, the night it started. The night her dying began.

chapter

1

There was a change coming, Laura knew there was. But what was it? A beginning or an end?

Either way, she'd be alone; she knew that now. And the thought made her shudder.

She tried to push it from her mind. She lifted her camera and looked through the viewfinder.

'Hurry up! I'm bloody freezing,' shouted Sarah, flapping her arms to keep warm.

'Nearly ready,' replied Laura, moving forward and adjusting one of the lamps to throw more light on the side of Sarah's face. She checked her viewfinder again.

'I think I heard that about an hour ago,' grumbled Sarah.

The thoughts refused to leave.

What will it be like, being alone?

Laura had never been alone before. They'd always been there for her. Ever since primary school, it had always been Sarah, Laura, Cass and Tina, 'the Four

Horsemen of the Potato Crisps,' inseparable and indi-
visible. But that was ending. They were drifting apart.

'OK, strike the pose.'

Sarah held her hands at face height, pushed her
arms forward and splayed her fingers, pointing long
false fingernails at the camera.

'And hold it ....'

'If we wait much longer, I won't have to hold it. I'll
be frozen like this.'

'And here we go.' Laura pushed the shutter release
and the Bronica whirred away, taking fourteen expo-
sures in rapid succession.

'And that's it.'

'About time too,' called Sarah, racing across the
lawn and into the kitchen.

Laura rewound the film, opened the camera and
tipped the film into her hand. As she walked around
the garden taking down her lights and backdrops, she
tried to think only of the job in hand. But it didn't work.

Were they drifting away from her or was she was
drifting away from them?

Either way, it hurt.

It wasn't just the way they teased her about being
'stuck in a rut' because of her taste in music. Or the
way they greeted her with 'Hey, look, Laura's going to
invade Poland — again,' when she turned up to meet
them wearing boots and combats from the army-surplus
store, instead of the brand-name leisurewear they wore.
She could handle that and come away smiling. What
really hurt was the fact that she couldn't talk to them
any more — not about things that really mattered.

She'd tried it with the powdered milk issue. They
just hadn't got it. Sarah's comment had said it all.

'Look, Laura. I *know* that the company that makes
this chocolate is dumping powdered milk on the Third

World. I *know* that kids are dying because their parents are making feed with unsterilised water. But how's us boycotting their products going to help anything?'

After that, Laura hadn't even bothered trying to explain why she'd got involved in the other issue groups at school — Greenpeace, Amnesty, Save the Whale, Children First .... They wouldn't want to know. They'd just call her 'Saint Laura of Assisi, saviour of the world' — again.

But tonight was different. Tonight she and Sarah were as close as they'd ever been. Tonight it was like old times again. Tonight ....

'Christ! Not again.'

Laura straightened up. The pain between her eyes was back. It had been coming and going all week. It wasn't very severe, and it didn't last all that long, but it was irritating. The previous night she'd felt it fourteen times and had had to leave badminton because of it.

She took a deep breath, closed her eyes and concentrated on the pain. Somewhere — probably in one of her mother's books on natural healing — she'd read that you can make pain disappear by visualising it being caressed by soft music. Laura didn't know if she believed that, but it was worth a try.

'I've got a pink Cadillac,
It's got fins at the back,
It's got leopard-skin seats and a polka-dot dash,' she sang silently.
'Yeah, I got style —
Babe, I got style.
So come on, pretty baby,
Won't you come for a ride,
Boogie-woogie with me
Down on Paradise Drive, all right ....'
OK, so it was soft, but it was all that came to mind; and

'Oh, don't tell me she's got you brainwashed too, Lar!'

'You know, you can be a real airhead sometimes,' Laura said sharply. 'Maybe if you spent more time in R.E. listening to what's being said, instead of trying to flash your legs at Conor, you'd realise that Miss O'Toole has spent the last few weeks talking about the new growth in spirituality, and saying pretty much the same things as my mom.'

'Ah, now,' giggled Sarah. 'You can't honestly expect me to spend time listening to that old bat.'

'"That old bat" is only five years older than we are. Remember, she was a sixth-year when we started secondary? And might I also remind you' — Laura dropped her voice to a whisper — 'we're just passing her house.'

'Whatever.' Sarah shrugged dismissively. 'Why would I listen to her when I can dream about Conor? God, he gets more gorgeous every day!'

Laura groaned, then laughed involuntarily. Sarah's crush on Conor just got bigger and bigger.

'You think so? I think he's just a bloody big ego on legs, myself.'

Sarah stopped and stared at her, unsmiling.

'But you don't really mean that, do you?' she said. 'Everyone knows you two have got something going on, secretly.'

'Yeah, right,' laughed Laura. 'Big time.'

'I'm serious,' said Sarah. 'You see him three times a week, and —'

'Yeah, twice at badminton practice and once he comes around for extra history tuition from Dad. Big deal! It's been like that for years.'

'But it's been different over the last few months, hasn't it? Be honest. It's obvious from the way he looks at you and —'

it worked. *I must remember to tell Dad I've found a new use for one of his songs.*

She bent down, folded the backdrops onto her cameras and lights, closed her camera case and stood up. Through the kitchen window, she could see her mother talking to Sarah.

Sarah looked beautiful. She always did. She was sitting with her legs wedged up against the heater. Her hands were wrapped around a cup of hot soup and she was wearing a baggy sweater and jeans, but she still looked beautiful. Laura shook her head. Even after two hours standing in the back garden, wearing a light cotton nightdress, posing as a ghost while Laura clicked away on her cameras and readjusted the lights, Sarah still managed to look as if she'd just stepped off the cover of *Vogue*.

She'd love that, Laura thought. *Modelling for* Vogue *or strutting the catwalks of Paris — that'd be her dream come true. God! What a waste!*

She was glad the others weren't there to hear that. She could almost hear their reaction. 'Wow! Talk about pretentious, élitist crap! Come off it, Laura.'

But if she was being pretentious or élitist, at least she didn't mean to be. If Sarah wanted to be a model — well, fair enough. But, personally, Laura could think of only one thing more futile than spending your life as a mobile clothes-horse, and that was spending your life photographing them. To her, photography was more important than that.

～

She couldn't say what had started it. Maybe it had been flicking through some old photo magazines at home and finding Robert Capa's famous photographs of the Spanish Civil War, or maybe it had been seeing the photo in her history book (photographer unknown) of the mother and baby waiting at the gates of a feeding camp in Zaïre. Laura wasn't sure. She just knew that sometime, a long time ago, she'd decided that her one ambition was to become a war photographer and take photographs like those.

The others thought she was nuts. For them, her photography was about the photos she took of them at school dances or sports days, and 'real photographers' were the ones who did photo shoots for *Vogue* or *Hello*, not the ones Laura liked.

She'd tried explaining it to them.

'Just think about the Vietnam War ....'

'We weren't born then.'

'No, but you've seen the photos in our history books: that Buddhist monk burning himself to death, the South Vietnamese officer shooting the communist prisoner through the head — and that famous one of the little girl running down the road naked, with napalm burning the skin off her back. And you've seen the photos that have come out of Rwanda and Bosnia and —'

'They're gross.'

'Yeah, but they're real. They show us what's happening around us. They make us think. Well, that's what I want to do with my babies. I want to take real photos that ....'

They couldn't understand. Maybe no one could. Maybe she was nuts.

~

She walked into the kitchen and put her camera case on the floor.

'Really, Lar,' her mother said, sounding annoyed. 'That was very unfair of you, keeping Sarah out there all that time. It's coming into winter, you know. She

could have got pneumonia. If I'd realise[d] out there, I'd have called you in hours ag[o]

'But Sash doesn't mind, do you, Sa[rah]' Laura. 'Anything for your art, isn't that ri[ght]

'Oh, absolutely, darlink,' sighed Sara[h] back of her hand against her forehead, clo[sing] and turning her head to one side in an [imitation of] some silent-movie-starlet swoon. 'I vould [die for my] art, darlink.'

'Just as well. With Laura as a friend, yo[u might] get the chance,' smiled Chris Byrne, turn[ing back to] her book.

Laura ladled herself a cup of soup and p[ut it on] the old pine table.

'Your mom's just been telling me all [about spirit] guides,' said Sarah, throwing her eyes up [to heaven] and shaking her head.

Laura glared at her angrily, but Sarah just [grinned.]

'We'd better go,' said Laura firmly. She sto[od up and] grabbed her coat from the back of the door.

'Bye, Chris,' said Sarah, following Laura's [lead.]

'Bye. Laura, don't be out too long.'

'I won't.' Laura grabbed two Mars ba[rs off the] counter and headed down the hall. Sarah w[as be]hind her, whistling.

She always has to do it, doesn't she? Things wi[ll be going] just fine, and then Sarah has to spoil it with one o[f her] remarks.

'Your mom's really cute,' said Sarah, as th[ey walked] out onto the avenue. 'The way she gets all caug[ht up in] that weird stuff ....'

'What weird stuff?' snapped Laura.

'You know — all this yoga and meditat[ion and sp]irit-guide stuff ....'

'What's weird about it?'

'You must be joking.'

'I'm not.'

Laura stared at Sarah. 'You really aren't joking, are you?' she said incredulously. 'You actually mean it.'

'Of course I mean it. Everyone knows you think of him as yours.'

'Oh, for God's sake, grow up! Anyone with half a brain would know better than that.'

Sarah just shrugged, unconvinced.

'Come on, Sash,' Laura said, almost pleading.

Sarah just stared at her.

'Oh, stuff you,' snapped Laura, turning away. 'Whatever you, Conor or anyone else might think or say ....'

Sarah put an arm around Laura's shoulders and burst out laughing.

'God, Lar, you're getting awful easy to wind up these days. I was only joking.'

Laura didn't believe her. But she wanted to, she really wanted to. There'd been too many times recently when she'd felt distanced from Sarah. So she laughed too.

'Bitch!'

They crossed the pavement and walked over to Sarah's gate.

'About my mom ....' began Laura.

'Hey! Laura!'

Neither of them had noticed the group of teenagers, boys and girls, slouching up the other side of the road.

'Oh God, here comes one of your fan club,' said Sarah, half smiling. 'For God's sake, don't let that bunch of scumbags come over here. You know how my old man hates them.'

'Even though you love them, of course,' said Laura sarcastically.

'Look, just get Gnasher away from here as quick as you can.'

Laura crossed the road. A long-haired boy with a mouthful of braces greeted her with a smile. His name was David Coyle, but most people called him Gnasher, after the cartoon dog in the *Beano*. He was holding a white plastic bag. The contents clinked softly as he put the bag on the ground.

'Laura, I was just wondering if you could lend us fifty pence to buy a Mars bar.'

Yeah, right, Laura thought. *More like a contribution towards the price of another can of lager.*

'Sorry, Dave. I haven't got a penny,' she said. 'But I'll tell you what I do have.' She put her hand into her coat pocket and pulled out the two Mars bars. 'Just for you!'

She flicked the two bars to one of the girls. The girl's name was Barbara Carolan, but even in the fading light you could see the hundreds of little brown marks on her face that had earned her her nickname: it had started off as Freckles, but over time that had been shortened to Eccles and then to Kelz.

'Thanks!' smiled Kelz, putting the bars in her pocket.

'And now you don't need fifty pence, do you?' laughed Laura.

'You're a bloody saint, Laura,' said Gnasher. 'You must be, having Superbitch for a mate.' He nodded towards Sarah, who was glaring at them across the road. 'Anyway, gotta go. See ya.'

He picked up his bag and the group slouched up the avenue, heading towards the field behind the school.

'See ya,' said Laura, crossing the road back to Sarah.

'What a bunch of morons,' sneered Sarah, watching them disappear up the avenue. 'It's half-ten on a Friday night, and they're off to sit in a field and freeze their bloody balls off while they get pissed. Losers!' She pushed the gate open with her foot.

'Oh, they're all right. You should try talking to them

sometime. Gnasher's a fabulous musician, and —'

'They're a bunch of scumbags,' said Sarah, cutting Laura off in mid-sentence. 'But, Jesus, Laura, you talk to anyone. I've even seen you looking at that weirdo, Declan Donnelly.'

'He's not weird, he's just quiet. And I'm dying to know where he was during his missing year, and —'

'Yeah, whatever,' interrupted Sarah. She turned and walked up the path. 'You won't forget you promised me six A4 copies of those photos, will you, Lar?'

'I doubt if you'd let me.'

'See you Monday,' Sarah called from her doorway.

Monday! A few weeks earlier, it would have been 'See you tomorrow afternoon' or 'I'll call for you tomorrow night.' Now it was 'Monday'!

Suddenly Laura was feeling angry — not with Sarah, with herself. She'd lost the chance to say something about Sarah's reaction to her mother. *Maybe I did it on purpose. Maybe not losing my friends is more important to me than being loyal to my family.*

Spineless wimp, she said to herself as she opened the front door. *Spineless bloody wimp.*

She rushed up to her room, pulled the little key from the chain around her neck and unlocked her diary.

Captain's Log
Friday, 13 October
10.45 p.m.

The pain in my head was back again tonight. It's driving me mad. But at least there's probably an easy cure for that. The question is, what do I do about

Sarah? I really hate her constant bloody sniping and put-downs. Part of me thinks I should just call it a day, forget about them and move on, but the other part's saying "Move on where? To who?' They're the only friends I've ever had.

Why is life so bloody complicated?

chapter

2

Captain's Log
Saturday, 21 October
11.05 p.m.

Dad showed me something from a Kinky Friedman book he was reading. "You can pick your nose, and you can pick your friends, but you can't wipe your friends off on the seat of your pants.' Well, maybe not on my pants, but after what happened tonight I certainly wouldn't mind wiping the others off somewhere. Jesus, they can be so pathetic!

The worst part is, I was only joking ....

~

It started with Gnasher.

As Laura was waiting for the bus to town, he strolled past with some of his friends. He slowed his pace to let the others move out of earshot.

'Hey, I'd watch that bitchy friend of yours,' he warned Laura, when no one else could hear. 'She's really after your pal Conor. I saw them down by the river the other night.'

Laura sighed wearily. Even Gnasher believed the school myth.

'Look, Dave. He's not my *pal*, as you call it. So they're free to do what they like.'

'Fair enough, but I just thought you should know.'

Later, when Laura met the others outside the cinema, she used Gnasher's comment as a throwaway line, a joke. But the humour was all one-sided.

'Well, guess who my spies tell me was down by the river with Conor last night?'

'Well, it wasn't me,' Sarah lied, angrily. 'And even if I was, what's it to you, if you don't care about him?'

'Yeah, Laura,' Cass joined in. 'You're always telling us you're not an item, so why get so upset?'

'Jesus, it was just a joke. Don't get so uptight.'

'If anyone's getting upset here, it's you,' Tina chipped in. 'Can't you take the competition?'

'Keep your shirt on. It was a *joke*.'

But the others were in no laughing mood. It was only later that Laura began to wonder if they'd been talking about her and Conor before she arrived. She decided they probably had.

'Anyway, if you do lose him it's your own fault,' snapped Sarah.

'How many times do I have to tell you there's nothing to lose? I'll give you a signed statement if you like.'

'God only knows what he sees in you anyway,' said

Tina nastily. 'You dress like something out of an old war movie, and all you can talk about are your bloody causes. What is it this week, Saint Laura? The rain forest or the one-winged Zambian butterfly?'

Laura felt her anger rising, but she wasn't going to give them the pleasure of seeing it. She just smiled.

'Maybe we'll talk again when you grow up.' She turned away and walked home alone.

~

She locked the diary and slipped it under her pillow.

Was this friendship? Jesus, if it was, what was it like to have enemies?

What a waste of a Saturday!

Laura wiped the tears from her eyes, picked up her Walkman, slipped the earphones on and pressed Play.

'Whatever you want,
Whatever you like,
Whatever you say,
You pay your money,
You take your choice ....' sang Status Quo.
'Whatever you need,
Whatever you use,
Whatever you win,
Whatever you lose ....' Laura sang along with them, quietly.

She fell back onto the bed, closed her eyes and let the music carry her along, between tears.

That was another difference between her and the others: music. The others thought the music she liked was, as Cass had put it, 'a pile of absolute crap'. Laura preferred to think of it as 'wide-ranging'. As far as she was concerned, everything had its place: Strauss, trad, jazz, Ray Charles, Abba, Boyzone, Status Quo .... She liked them all, for different times, different moods.

Tonight was definitely a Status Quo night.

'Ah, here we are and here we are and here we go,' sang Francis Rossie and Rick Parfitt.

'Fireball and we're hitting the road,' Laura sang along.

'Here we go-o,
Rockin' all over the world ....'

'Sanjid — my name is Sanjid. Is anybody listening?'

Laura sat bolt upright The voice had hit her right between the eyes, with a stinging sensation.

'What the hell?'

It had been weak and muffled, as if someone was speaking through a scarf, but it had definitely been there.

She stopped the tape, rewound, and hit Play.

'Here we go-o,
Rockin' all over the world ....'

'Sanjid — my name is Sanjid. Is anybody listening?'

It was still there, but this time there wasn't any pain.

'Kev!' Laura snapped angrily.

She hit the Stop button, snatched the tape out of the Walkman and rushed across the hall to Kevin's room.

'What the hell do you think you're playing at?' she demanded, waving the tape at him. 'Ruining my tape like that!'

'I wouldn't touch your poxy tapes,' sniffed Kev, looking up from the latest issue of the *X-Men* comic.

'No? Well, what do you call this — Sanjid!'

Laura slid the tape into his stereo and rewound it.

'Personally, I call it a load of old crap,' shrugged Kev, as the sound of Status Quo came blasting through the speakers. 'What do you call it, high art?'

The song played all the way to the end, without interference. The voice wasn't there.

I couldn't have imagined it. Not twice.

Laura rewound the tape again.

'If you have to play music in here, at least put on something decent,' snorted Kev.

Laura ignored him and listened carefully to the tape. There was nothing there; just Status Quo. It had to be one of Kev's tricks.

She snatched the tape out of the stereo. 'I don't know how you did that,' she shouted over her shoulder as she stormed out of the room, 'but you play around with my tapes any more and I'll kill you.'

'Do come for another visit real soon,' Kev called after her, adding under his breath, 'Prat!'

Laura put the tape back into her Walkman and listened. It was just Status Quo.

I'll find out what he did if it kills me. Christ! Why do brothers have to be such a pain?

She flopped back onto her bed and closed her eyes.

'I like it, I like it, I la-la-la-like it, la-la-la-like it,' she sang along with Francis Rossie and Rick Parfitt.

'Here we go-o,
Rockin' all over the world ....'

~

Captain's Log (Supplemental)
Saturday, 21 October
11:30 p.m.

I don't know how he did it, but if Kev doesn't stop fooling with my tapes I'll wring his sorry little neck. Where'd he come up with a name like Sanjid? It's a bit exotic for him. I would've thought Dickhead would be more appropriate.

chapter 3

Laura looked down at what she'd written.

Captain's Log
Sunday, 22 October
10.15 p.m.

I still haven't found out how he does it, but I'm sure it's Kev, although after lunch-time I can't be 100% certain. But it has to be him. There can't be another answer.

That wasn't the truth. She knew it. Even before she'd put the last full stop on the page, she knew she wasn't telling the truth. There was another answer. She just didn't want to accept it.

～

The voice had called her four times.

The first time she had been in the shower.

'Sanjid — my name is Sanjid. Is anybody listening?'

She wasn't sure. She'd felt the stinging between her eyes and thought she'd heard something, faint and indistinct, but she wasn't sure.

The second time she'd been drying herself.

'Sanjid — my name is Sanjid. Is anybody listening?'

The house was perfectly silent and she knew she'd heard it. It still sounded like someone talking through a scarf, but it was definitely a voice.

She pulled the towel around her and marched into Kev's room.

'Kev, knock it off. It's not funny.'

Kev rolled over, snoring.

'Have it your own way. I'll get you yet.'

Kev carried on snoring.

The third time there was no mistaking it. It was a voice. Someone had removed the scarf, and it was loud and clear.

'Sanjid — my name is Sanjid. Is anybody listening?'

Laura jumped, nearly knocking Sunday brunch all over the floor of the Harcourt Hotel.

'What was that all about?' moaned Kev, steadying the table. Laura didn't reply. On stage, Niall Toner Jr was still singing.

'I got home about quarter to four,
Met the milkman at the door,
Ain't goin' dancin' any more
Doin' the Dublin two-step
Doin' the Dublin two-step ....'

'Sanjid — my name is Sanjid,' the voice called again. *'Is anybody listening?'*

Laura gasped, 'Oh God.' She felt faint. She felt dizzy. The life suddenly seemed to drain out of her body. Now that the voice was clearer, it sounded nothing like Kev's. It was higher and younger, more like Katie's, but it couldn't be Katie; she was downstairs in the toilet. And it definitely wasn't Kev. His lips hadn't moved. And even if somehow he had managed to throw his voice, someone else would have heard; but their mother was right beside Laura, and she hadn't said a word. The only other person who would have played a trick like that was her father, and he was on stage playing harmonica with the band.

'Are you OK?' asked Kev. 'You've gone pure white.'

Laura didn't reply. She felt her breathing becoming strained and shallow.

'Mom, Laura needs her inhaler.' Kev reached quickly for his mother's handbag, opened it, grabbed the inhaler and passed it to Laura. She placed the nozzle in her mouth and pressed. The cool, chalky-tasting spray hit the back of her throat.

'Are you bad?' asked Chris.

Laura shook her head. She didn't want to have to explain.

'Maybe you should go outside for a while. It's a bit smoky in here.'

Laura took another deep breath and pressed the inhaler again.

'Do you want me to come?'

Laura stood up and shook her head. As she made her way to the street, she could hear Niall Toner Sr singing,

'From New Orleans to Nantucket,

Kicked the safe and kicked the bucket,

Jack Daniels was a whiskey-drinking man ....'

as her father wailed away on his harmonica.

She sat on the hotel steps, watching the Sunday lunch-time traffic flow down Harcourt Street. Her breathing was beginning to ease, but her mind was going into free fall.

Before, she'd been convinced that the voice was one of Kev's tricks. Now she knew it couldn't be.

Maybe it had been Niall Jr joining in one of Kev's little pranks? But she'd been looking at him, and singing along, as he sang:

'I went dancing down to Templebar,
To see my favourite country star.
Think that he'll be going far,
Doin' the Dublin two-step
Doin' the Dublin two-step ....'

That was when it had happened: right on the instrumental break. And it couldn't have been Katie, or Chris, or Joe. And it had come straight into that place in the middle of her forehead where she'd been hearing the buzzing for weeks. And ....

Oh God, please, no.

An answer to the question she wouldn't ask had presented itself. Laura shivered and hugged herself tight.

Not a Mrs Bradley. Please, not a Mrs Bradley.

She felt like crying, but she couldn't. Tears would require an explanation, and she didn't have one; at least, not one that didn't frighten her.

~

Shakespeare first spoke to Mrs Bradley as she was peering into the supermarket deep-freeze, trying to decide between a small frozen pizza and a small frozen turkey; not that it really mattered that much, not since her husband had gone to Lebanon with the United Nations. There'd only been the two of them, and dinner

wasn't much of an event now that it was just her and
the dog in a little basement flat.

'I'd recommend the pizza,' said Shakespeare. 'So much
more romantic than a dead bird, don't you think?'

Mrs Bradley thought the Bard of Avon's reasoning
was perfectly logical. So she opted for the pizza, pep-
peroni with extra mozzarella. After that, Shakespeare
began visiting her regularly, offering her advice on
hairstyles, clothes, reading material. He even read to
her from his previously unknown works — sonnets,
plays, a musical based on the life of Saddam Hussein.

Mrs Bradley took great delight in telling her first-
year history class all about their little chats. They began
as occasional encounters, but soon they became weekly,
then daily, and finally hourly events. The first-years
found the chats considerably more interesting than Mrs
Bradley's string-of-dates approach to teaching history.

Then it happened.

Right at the start of the first period after lunch,
Shakespeare brought some of his literary contemporar-
ies to meet Mrs Bradley. These gentlemen, she
announced proudly, pointing to her empty chair, were
some of the finest minds in Elizabethan England: Ben
Jonson, Kit Marlowe and Francis Bacon. For some
reason, Mrs Bradley took an immediate dislike to
Bacon. As the first-years watched with interest, she
began a rather heated debate with the dead writer —
who, if one followed her stare, seemed to have moved
from the teacher's chair to a spot just above the classroom door.

At first the disagreement was fairly controlled, with
Mrs Bradley shaking her head and saying politely, 'I
can't agree with that' and 'I beg to differ there.' Then it
all changed.

Her face became redder and redder. Before anyone could say 'Please, Miss, it's break-time,' she exploded in a fury, hurling chairs and books against the door-frame, screaming.

'A writer! You a serious *writer*! Don't make me fucking laugh. You're just a talentless little shit, with less creativity than the great Bard's piss!'

Eventually, the first-years were rescued from the debate by Mrs Maguire and the headmaster. A little while later the ambulance came.

Mrs Bradley never returned to the school. Laura saw her sometimes, walking around the streets as if she were in a trance, staring straight ahead with big, dead eyes. Laura had heard all sorts of phrases being thrown around: ECT, frontal lobotomy .... She thought Gnasher's comment — 'Uppers for breakfast, downers for dinner and knockout drops for supper' — was probably closest to the truth.

She couldn't possibly be heading down the same route as Mrs Bradley, could she?

～

Since they'd arrived home from the Harcourt she'd been in bed, trying to sleep. She was terrified the voice would come back, and sleeping was the only way she could think of to avoid it. But she couldn't sleep. She just lay there, staring at the ceiling, remembering the voice and thinking about Mrs Bradley; poor, sweet, lonely Mrs Bradley.

Oh God!

She closed her diary and put it under her pillow.

'Sanjid — my name is Sanjid. Is anybody listening?'

The voice was so clear that it might have been right beside her.

Laura froze. Her breathing stopped and her mind

blanked completely. There was no thought, no picture, just blackness.

'I'm Sanjid from Bihar. Is anybody listening?'

The blackness seemed to go on forever. Then panic forced her mouth open and she gasped, filling her lungs with cool fresh air. Her breathing eased, then began to slow.

Bewar!

The word suddenly erupted in her mind. The voice had said, 'I am Sanjid from Bewar.'

Laura had never heard of 'Bewar'.

Could you go mad and hear people talking about places you'd never heard of?

Laura pushed herself out of bed and pulled on her dressing-gown. If Bewar was real, then maybe she wasn't going mad; maybe something else was happening. She didn't know what that could be, but if she could find Bewar maybe she would have the answer.

Or maybe she was just clutching at straws. She didn't know, but she had to find out.

She raced down the stairs two at a time. In the front room, her parents were watching another rerun of *Hill Street Blues* on television. Katie was curled up on the sofa, asleep.

Laura felt a strong urge to tell them everything that was happening, all about the voice and Bewar or whatever it was called — everything. But she didn't. She remembered Mrs Bradley.

'How are you feeling now?' asked Chris, as Laura poked her head around the door.

'Oh, I'm all right,' she fibbed.

'Are you sure?' asked her father. 'You weren't great today.'

'Oh, I'm fine, really fine,' Laura said, forcing herself to smile. 'But I've just remembered something we were talking about in school. Has either of you ever heard of anywhere called Bewar, or something like that?'

'Bewar,' Joe repeated. 'Bewar. Sounds sort of familiar. Any ideas, Chris?'

'Isn't it in Afghanistan or Thailand or somewhere in the East?' offered his wife.

'Could be,' he said. 'It does sound sort of familiar. Why not try the encyclopaedias?'

~

The encyclopaedias were housed in what Joe called 'the study' and Chris called 'the garage'. The room had been a garage when the Byrnes first moved in, but Joe had had it converted into a room and stuck in a few bookshelves, a couple of chairs and an old table. Now he called it the study. Chris could never get used to that idea; to her it was still the garage.

Laura switched the light on. The room was cold. It always was — a testimony to the poor workmanship of the fellow who'd converted it.

The encyclopaedias were lined up against the far wall. Laura picked up Volume A, sat down in the old rocking-chair and switched on the electric fire. She skimmed through the pages, reading highlights, her eye searching for anything that sounded or looked even vaguely like 'Bewar'.

She was feeling slightly less frightened. If her parents thought they'd heard of it, then it probably did exist; and if it existed, then she might not be going mad.

By the time she replaced Volume A with T, she felt ready to write a school project on Afghanistan. It was all very interesting, but she hadn't found any mention of a Bewar, Biar, Byhar, or anything remotely like that. She was no closer when she'd finished looking through Thailand.

'Find anything?' asked Joe, poking his head around the door.

Laura shook her head.

'Try Africa. It does sound familiar, honest. We're off to bed. Don't stay up too late.'

'I won't.'

Laura took out Volume A again and flicked through the pages until she came to Africa.

'Bloody hell.'

There were forty-two pages on Africa. If she was going to read that, Laura decided, she might as well get comfortable. She moved to the living-room, grabbing her father's overcoat off the coat-stand on the way. She fluffed up two cushions and put them on the corner of the sofa. Then she pulled her dressing-gown close around her and curled up on the sofa, under the overcoat.

AFRICA

Area: 11,707,000 sq. miles
Population: 452,000,000 (in 1979)
The second largest of the continents (only Asia has a greater area), Africa ranks third in population, after Asia and Europe. In 1950 only four African countries were independent. Since then ....

chapter

4

Laura woke to the shrill sound of the telephone. She kicked off the duvet and raced down the hall.

'Hello?'

'Hi, sleepy-head! It's me.'

'Mom! Where are you?'

'I'm in work. I just thought I'd phone and wake you before you slept the day away.'

'Work!' said Laura in surprise. 'What time is it?'

'A couple of minutes before noon.'

'Why didn't you wake me for school?'

'I thought about it, but you looked so comfortable. Anyway, you had a rough day yesterday, and God knows what time you stayed up till last night. So I just replaced Joe's overcoat with the duvet and left you.'

'You were probably right,' Laura admitted. 'I have no idea what time I fell asleep.'

She suddenly became aware of voices, women and children screaming, at the other end of the phone.

'Oops! Looks like we're going to have another day of fun and games here at the refuge,' said Chris quickly. 'I'd better go. There's a note on the table. See you about four. Bye.'

The phone went dead.

Laura went down to the kitchen and picked up the note.

'Laura was late for school today as she had an asthma attack yesterday. Chris Byrne.'

It was near enough to the truth.

Laura yawned and poured herself a bowl of corn-flakes. She was now the world's greatest expert on Africa, Thailand, Afghanistan and Indonesia — she'd thrown that one in on a hunch — but she was still no closer to finding Bewar or Biyar or whatever it was called, presuming it existed. And it had to exist. Both of her parents seemed sure it did.

Funny: she didn't feel anywhere near as panicky or excited about it as she had the night before. Maybe she was just too tired, or maybe she'd used up all her emotion.

Was that how it had been for Mrs Bradley? Periods of confusion, panic, excitement — and then nothing, just normality?

Laura finished her cereal, ran upstairs and dressed in double-quick time. Sarah and Conor were debating against Anne Heany and Jane Cousant at twelve-thirty. She'd promised to be there to give them moral support, and, even if she wasn't feeling too loyal to Sarah after the events of the weekend, she wouldn't break a promise.

She raced downstairs, grabbed her coat and opened the front door, checking to make sure she had her key.

'*Sanjid — my name is Sanjid. Is anybody listening?*'

The voice was perfectly clear. It came to a spot right

in the centre of her forehead, like a soft throbbing.
Laura slammed the door.

'Oh, please, not again. Not again,' she pleaded,
clenching her fists and closing her eyes. 'Please just
piss off and leave me alone. I don't want to go mad.'

'What's pissoff?' asked the voice softly. 'Does it
mean go away?'

Laura took a breath, pulling the air deep into her
stomach, then exhaled through her nose, filling her
mind with a loud 'ummm' sound. It was her approxi-
mation of something she'd heard her mother do during
meditation. It would make the voice go away.

'That's not the *om*,' said the voice. 'I've heard the sa-
cred *om* sound. That isn't it.'

'Please piss off,' Laura pleaded again, filling her mind
with the sound. 'Go away. I don't want to go mad.'

'What's making you mad?'

'You,' she said loudly. 'You. The stupid little voice in
my head.'

'Why am I stupid?' asked the voice.

'Because you're not real,' Laura said, closing her
eyes tighter. 'You're just some sort of bloody illusion or
something.'

She started to run. Maybe if she ran fast enough she
could outrun the voice ....

The voice inside her head giggled, a gentle, high-
pitched giggle, like Katie laughing in her sleep.

'Don't be scared. I'm real. I'm Sanjid.'

'Yeah, and I'm Joan of Arc,' hissed Laura.

'Oh, so that's your name! Joan of Arc,' said the voice.

'No! I'm Laura, *Laura*, and —'

'I'm Sanjid. Can I be your friend?'

'I have enough friends, thank you!'

'Let me be your friend, Laura.'

'Look. Just leave me alone. Please leave ....' Laura

clenched her hands in front of her and looked up pleadingly, as if the voice was coming from someone in the sky above her. 'Just please ....'

Sarah's face was pressed against the window of one of the upstairs classrooms.

'Oh God,' groaned Laura. She was standing in the middle of the school playground. Without being aware of it, she had run to school.

'Now look what you've done,' she whispered to herself, raising her hand and smiling up at Sarah. 'They'll be fetching the little men in the white coats for me soon, if I'm not careful.'

'What little men?' asked the voice in her head.

'Go away, please, please,' Laura screamed silently, as she rushed into school and down the corridor into the girls' toilets. 'Go away.'

'I don't want you to send me away,' pleaded the little voice. 'Please. I just want to talk, be your fr —'

Something crashed, hard, against the side of Laura's face. She screamed and stumbled backwards, sprawling on the floor, expecting to see someone coming out of one of the cubicles in a flurry of apologies for having opened the door too fast. There was no one there.

Laura looked up at the ceiling. Maybe a tile or a fitting had fallen and hit her.

Nothing.

She pulled herself off the floor, holding on to one of the wash-basins.

'Oh, no!'

The right side of her face was a swollen, angry mass of red and blue bruises. Her eye was closing, and blood was pouring from her mouth.

'Jesus —'

She wiped at her mouth with the back of her hand. Instinctively, she looked down. There was nothing there. Apart from the dampness of her own saliva, her hand was dry.

She looked back at the mirror. The blood was gone, and the bruises and swellings were disappearing before her eyes.

'Oh, Christ, what's happening to me?'

Laura's stomach was heaving with fear. She made it to a cubicle just in time. Bending over the toilet bowl, she heaved again and again, until at last she was dry-retching.

'Oh, God, don't let me be going crazy. Please,' she sobbed, trembling. 'Please.'

She tore some toilet paper from the roll and wiped her mouth and her eyes, then collapsed onto the toilet seat.

'I'm sorry, Laura,' the little voice in her head said tearfully. 'I didn't mean you to feel that, but he sneaked up on me and hit me with a lump of wood because I missed a line.'

'W-w-what ....' stuttered Laura incoherently.

'I must go, but I'll come back,' the voice said sadly.

Laura felt the middle of her forehead, where the throbbing had been, relax.

'Sweet Jesus. What's —'

The door to the girls' toilets slammed open.

'Did you see her?' asked Sarah, laughing.

'Who?' asked Tina.

'Laura!' laughed Sarah. 'Laura.'

'What's she done now?' sighed Cass wearily.

Laura sat upright. For a second she thought Sarah had heard her and was making some sort of joke.

'God, I know Laura's always been a bit weird —'

'You can say that again,' said Tina.

'But I think she's losing it completely,' Sarah continued. 'A few minutes ago she was walking across the playground, waving her arms around and talking to herself.'

'That sounds a bit serious,' said Cass. 'Maybe we should see if we can find her, in case she's going a bit Mrs Bradley and does something stupid or —'

'We're not her babysitters, you know,' said Sarah firmly. 'And she's not even one of us any more, not really. So if she's losing it, it's not our problem.'

'Suppose you're right,' said Cass, sounding less than convinced.

'Go on, admit it. You just don't want Conor seeing you hanging around with a looper,' teased Tina.

Laura heard them laughing, heard the sound of running water, paper towels being torn from the dispenser and thrown into the bin.

'I just hope she manages to keep out of her straitjacket long enough to come to the debate and vote for us,' laughed Sarah, as the main door creaked open.

'Yeah, and if her invisible friend votes as well that'll be two votes,' giggled Tina.

The door slammed shut behind them.

Laura felt numbed. Suddenly, it was all too much for her: the voice, the blow in the face, the bruising and the blood, and now this .... Tears rolled down her face.

'I'm going mad,' she sobbed. 'And all my so-called friends can do is laugh at me. It's not fair. Those bloody bitches! It's not fair.'

The tears flooded down her cheeks, dribbling onto her hands. Her whole body trembled as she sobbed, silent little sobs that caught in her throat.

The door slammed open again. A rush of girls came clattering in, kicking open the door of each cubicle in turn.

'Get lost!' screamed Laura as someone kicked her door.

'Or else?' challenged a voice.

'Just go away and leave me alone,' Laura pleaded.

'Or else?' it repeated, as a head suddenly appeared above the partition to Laura's right. 'Or — Christ, Laura, are you OK? What's up?' asked Kelz, her tone changing instantly from aggression to concern.

'I'm OK,' said Laura softly. 'It's just ....'

'I didn't realise it was you, Laura. Otherwise I wouldn't have gone shooting my mouth off and —'

'It's OK,' replied Laura. She stood up, wiped her eyes on her sleeve and came out of the cubicle.

Kelz jumped down from the partition and joined her. Some of the other girls from Gnasher's crowd were standing around, cigarettes in their hands.

'Are you sure you're all right?' one of them asked. 'Only your eyes are all red and you look like shit.'

'No, I'm fine, really,' said Laura. She turned on the tap and splashed cool, fresh water on her face. She felt completely drained. There was an emptiness where her stomach should have been. She just wanted to be alone.

Kelz pulled a paper towel from the dispenser and handed it to her, leaning back against the wash-basin.

'Was it Superbitch?' she asked angrily. 'We just saw her and the other two walking out of here. If they did anything to you, we'll ....'

'It's OK.' Laura smiled. 'I'm just feeling lousy and sick. That time!' she lied. 'That time.'

'What a drag.'

Kelz moved so close to Laura that their faces almost touched. 'Only if it is them — I mean, I know you hang around with them and all —'

'*Hung* around with them,' Laura corrected.

'Whatever. The thing is, you're not like them. You never were, even when we were little. You were never a snobby bitch, Laura. So if they did anything to you ....'

Kelz turned quickly and delivered a perfect high ka-rate kick to the top of the cubicle door. Laura stared in surprise.

'I've been doing karate since I was seven,' smiled Kelz, a little embarrassed. 'My dad thinks every girl should know how to protect herself these days.'

'That's why we hang around with her,' laughed one of the others. 'She protects us from all harm.'

Kelz stuck her tongue out at them, then turned back to Laura. 'I mean it. If they did anything to you ....' she repeated.

'I appreciate it.' Laura smiled. It was nice to have a protector. 'But it's nothing like that.'

She looked at her watch. It was almost twenty-five to one.

'Aren't you going to the debate?' she asked, just for something to say.

'We thought we'd give it a miss this time,' said one of the girls, jumping up onto the low windowsill and lighting her cigarette.

'Tell Gnasher we were going to make it, but, well ....' started Kelz.

'All got detention,' called the girl who was blowing her smoke through the opened window.

'Yeah. He'd believe that,' laughed one of the others.

Laura nodded.

∼

It was all too much — Sanjid, the girls, everything. Laura just wanted to crawl into bed and stay there forever, but she knew she couldn't. She couldn't allow herself to fall apart. She had to try to ... what? She didn't know.

From down the corridor she heard Sarah's voice. 'And what we're trying to say is ....' The debate had already started. Laura peeped through the window. Sarah was talking, waving her hands around like a demented conductor. Cass was beckoning Laura to come in, moving up to make room for her. Automatically Laura opened the door and walked in.

Sarah looked up, smiled, and gave her a thumbs-up sign as if nothing had happened.

Suddenly Laura was fighting to control her anger.

Stuff you, she screamed silently. *Stuff the lot of you. You're nothing but a bunch of hypocrites. That was the last bloody straw.*

'Ah, stuff it!' she said loudly, turning around. 'They aren't worth the trouble.'

Sarah stopped speaking.

'I'm sorry, Laura, did you say something?' asked the chairman.

'Sorry,' laughed Laura, looking at Sarah. 'Wrong room. I was looking for a couple of friends, but they're not here.'

She closed the door behind her with a bang.

They were supposed to be her *friends*! They didn't even know the meaning of the word. They were two-faced bitches — all smiles to her face, but as nasty and vicious as hell when they thought she couldn't hear.

Through the window Laura saw Sarah's bewildered stare following her down the corridor.

'Stuff 'em,' she said again. She started giggling to herself. 'Stuff 'em! Stuff 'em ....'

Then she stopped. 'They're not even worth getting angry about.'

She sat down on the stairs to the library, closed her eyes, and started a relaxation technique her mother had taught her. Placing the backs of her hands on her knees, she curled the thumb and index finger of each hand together and breathed slowly and deeply, breathing in for a count of five, holding for five, and then breathing out for five. She repeated the exercise for a few minutes. When she stood up she was feeling a lot calmer.

As she pushed the library door open, Laura was aware that her anger was almost gone. The disappointment and the feeling of betrayal were still there, but she wasn't angry any more.

It had finally happened. Their friendship was over, gone forever. Laura would never have wanted it to end that way, but it had. She was no longer part of their little crowd. She would no longer have to deny the things that were important to her just because the others weren't interested.

She'd be polite. If they spoke to her, she'd answer. But she'd never start a conversation with them again, never have any feelings of friendship towards them; never trust them.

She closed the library door behind her. She'd spent enough time thinking about it. She had something more important to do.

chapter

5

Mrs Taylor, the librarian, was fingering through the
index cards on her desk. As Laura approached, she
looked up and smiled.

'Please tell me you want something terribly interesting and hard to find,' she said, with a warm chuckle in
her voice. 'That's what I need — something to take me
away from this for a while, before I go completely gaga.'

'I'm looking for a place — at least, I think it's a place
— that sounds like Beare, or Bewar, or something like
that.'

'Sounds exotic,' smiled Mrs Taylor, delightedly placing
her cards back in the filing box. 'Let's try the big atlas.'
She took off her glasses and let them dangle from the
chain around her neck.

Laura followed her to the shelves and watched in
admiration as the little librarian deftly took a book
about half her own size from the top shelf and placed it
noiselessly on the table.

'First we'll try the index.' Mrs Taylor opened the atlas at the back and ran a practised finger down the B listings.

'Beare, Bewar, something like that — let's see .... Do you have a pen and a piece of paper handy?'

Laura nodded.

'OK, got one,' said Mrs Taylor brightly. 'Beawar, India — page 88, grid Dc.'

Laura jotted down the reference.

'Bejar, Spain,' said Mrs Taylor, turning over the page. 'Bihar State, India; Bijar, Iran; Bijawar, India. Which one will we go for?'

Bihar — that was what the voice had been saying to her, not Bewar or Beare. Bihar!

'Bihar,' said Laura excitedly. 'Bihar State.'

It existed. It was real. She wanted to jump and scream and grab the little librarian and dance her up and down the room.

Mrs Taylor flicked through the pages of the atlas and ran a practised finger across the grid.

'There she is. Bihar; Bangladesh to the east, Bengal to the south.'

Laura looked at the square, taking in all the names. There it was: Bihar! She let out a long, deep sigh of pure joy. *This must be how Columbus felt when he finally found land.*

As she looked at the map, she found her attention drawn to a point west of Bihar.

'And what's this place?'

'The holy city of Varanasi,' said Mrs Taylor, following her glance. 'Formerly known as —'

Laura shook her head. 'No, this place. I can't read it.'

The librarian lifted her glasses to her eyes and moved her face closer to the page.

'My eyes aren't quite as young as they used to be,'

she chuckled. 'Is this the place? Mirzapur?'

Laura nodded.

'Can't say I know anything about it, but it sounds quite familiar for some reason. Try the encyclopaedia.' She picked up the atlas.

'It's OK,' Laura said. 'I'll put it back.'

'Thanks. I'd better get back to purgatory,' said Mrs Taylor, nodding at the filing cards.

Laura lifted down the encyclopaedia and flicked to India, scanning the pages and jotting down points as she searched for Bihar. She could have kissed Mrs Taylor.

INDIA

- *Seventh largest country in the world.*
- *1/7 of the world's population lives in India.*
- *Population = that of all the nations of Africa and South America put together.*
- *Many races and religions. 180 different languages, 14 major tongues and more than 700 dialects.*
- *Some people are very wealthy. Many others have only a few pennies a day. Some are forced to live on the streets. Average income = £60 a year.*
- *Twenty-two states (one of which is Bihar. Thank God). Eight territories (whatever they are).*
- *80% of the people live in rural areas.*
- *Over 232,000 villages, most with 1000 or fewer people living there.*
- *Only 2% of the people speak English.*

Laura put her pencil down, still almost shaking with excitement. Bihar existed. It was a state in India. Of course, that didn't prove she wasn't going mad, but .... She pushed the thought from her mind and looked at the list of facts in front of her.

'OK. What can I say about him from all this?'

She was surprised to hear herself say it so casually. But if Bihar was real, then maybe Sanjid was real; and if Sanjid was real, she had somehow made some sort of link with a kid halfway across the world ....

God, she hoped so. It was so much better than the alternative.

She read over her notes carefully.

Something wasn't quite right. What was it?

Laura stared at the page, almost willing the inconsistency to identify itself. Then she saw it.

'Some people are very wealthy. Many others have only a few pennies a day .... Only 2% of the people speak English.'

If only two percent of the population spoke English, it was a safe bet that they weren't the ones living in poverty. They would be the wealthy, the élite. But Sanjid spoke English. That would make him one of the wealthy.

It didn't fit.

The bell for the start of classes interrupted Laura's train of thought. She put the encyclopaedia on the shelf and slipped her notebook into her pocket.

'Did you find anything on Mirzapur?' asked Mrs Taylor, looking up from the index cards.

Laura shook her head.

'I'll tell you what. I'll ask my husband if you like. He's an economist, and I'm sure he could find something about it in one of those economic abstracts he's always reading.'

'That would be really nice of you,' said Laura, picking up her bag. 'Bye.'

'Bye. See you later.'

~

Laura stared at her art project, a rough shape consisting of a large cigar-shaped body and wings made from baked dough, which would eventually become a sculpture of a butterfly. She'd hardly touched it all afternoon. She couldn't concentrate. All she could think about was a boy in India talking to her in her head.

It didn't make sense. She wasn't telepathic — at least, she didn't think she was. And anyway, did being telepathic mean you could hold full conversations mentally? Surely it just meant you could read someone else's thoughts?

A couple of times, Laura noticed Declan Donnelly watching her.

Wonder if he knows anything about telepathy?

She was tempted to ask him, but in the end she decided not to. After all, she didn't know him that well.

He'd been a sixth-year, two years ahead of Laura, when he'd suddenly disappeared. No one had the slightest idea what had happened to him. There'd been rumours, of course: he'd joined a cult, had a nervous breakdown, entered a seminary. But no one really knew, and Declan never spoke about it.

When he'd returned to school, he'd joined Laura's year to start the two-year exam course all over again. Before his disappearance, he'd been an inter-county basketball player and had been offered a sports scholarship to some American university. Since his return he'd given up sports, cut himself off from his old friends and become a real loner.

Laura was longing to talk to him, to ask about that

year, but so far the closest they'd got to a conversation was 'Hello'.

~

When Laura got home, she went straight to the bookshelves in the study. She was sure there'd be something on telepathy there; and she was right. She found two books on unexplained phenomena wedged between a collection of 1960s Birmingham City F.C. match programmes (her father's) and two bound collections of *New Society* and *Social Work Today* (her mother's). She thanked God that her parents never threw a book out.

She skimmed the index for references to telepathy, flicked quickly to the relevant pages and read the articles. It was interesting stuff — she hadn't realised telepathic experiences were so common — but, unfortunately, nothing she read was related to what was happening to her. The closest thing was an account of studies on direct transmission, where subjects demonstrated an ability to send telepathic messages to one another at will. But it wasn't the same. They weren't holding ongoing telepathic conversations.

Maybe I am going mad. Maybe it's all a delusion.

~

'Did either of you ever hear of people being able to carry on conversations telepathically?' Laura asked her parents at tea-time.

'Well, only in sci-fi,' replied her father. 'Why? Are you thinking of trying?'

Laura just smiled.

'It'd certainly cut down on the phone bill,' Chris chipped in.

'No, it's a serious question.'

'OK, then, a serious answer,' said Joe. 'I know one of

the other teachers found an article on the Internet called "Telepathy in Two Minds". It was about the sort of thing you're talking about. It sounded a bit waffly, but I can find it for you if you like.'

'That'd be great.'

'There was an *X-Files* episode like that,' said Kev. 'All about this girl who could see what another girl was seeing.'

'I remember that,' Katie joined in. 'One girl was being cut and the other one was bleeding. It was great. They were in water, and ....'

~

Captain's Log
Monday, 23 October
10.45 p.m.

What a day! Sarah showed herself to be a real bitch. So did the others. That's it. As far as I'm concerned they're now my ex-friends. I've gone solo. Funny, though: I don't mind half as much as I thought I would. That's probably because of this Sanjid thing. Either I'm going crazy or I'm telepathic. Either way, I sound like something out of Kev and Katie's beloved X-Files.

At least I found Bihar. There's still something not quite right about that, but at least that bloody buzzing and aching has stopped.

chapter

6

Laura was surprised at how easy it was to get through two days without the others. They didn't have any classes together on Monday afternoon or Tuesday, so the next time she saw them was on Wednesday morning.

'What was that all about on Monday?' Sarah demanded as Laura came in for registration.

'What?'

'Your disappearing act.'

'I had more important things to do.'

'But you were supposed to come and vote for us.'

'I never said I'd vote for you. I said I'd go and vote on the argument, but I changed my mind.'

'Well, thanks a lot,' said Sarah angrily. 'We lost by one bloody vote, thanks to you.'

Laura shook her head slowly, without betraying any emotion. 'If you lost, it was because the others were better,' she said matter-of-factly.

'That's cool, babe,' said Conor, patting an empty

seat beside him. 'Just slide your sweet self over here.'

'Dream on, dickhead.' Laura turned away and walked to the back of the class.

'We lost,' Sarah shouted after her, 'because we needed one bloody vote.'

Laura shrugged. '*Que sera sera*. What will be, will be.'

As she said it, she noticed Declan Donnelly smiling and quietly nodding.

She'd heard from some of the other kids in her art class that, at the end of the debate, he'd made a speech from the floor which had completely demolished Sarah's and Conor's argument. The only reason they hadn't lost by a landslide was that the debate had been packed with their friends. Laura smiled back at Declan.

She sat at an empty desk, opened her notebook and looked over her notes on India. She had a lot of information, most of it from a file of Third-World-related press clippings she'd found on the bookshelves in the study. It made grim reading.

In India, luxury existed side by side with appalling deprivation and poverty. Millions of Indians survived by selling the labour of the entire family, parents and children, to the local stone quarries, firework factories, glass factories, or large farms. Millions more survived by subsistence farming, scratching an existence from small family plots that could be wiped out at any moment if the weather went against them. When that happened, many were left with little alternative but to move into the cities, live on the streets, and beg or become rag-pickers, scavenging through rubbish tips to see what they could find to sell.

And then there were the moneylenders. They seemed to be everywhere in Indian society, lending money at such astronomically high interest rates that, in many cases, the loans could never be repaid; debts

would pass from father to son and on to grandson.
Because of the moneylenders, whole generations were
born into debt. Many of the people who worked in the
quarries, the mines, and the factories were doing so to
pay off debts that, in reality, would never be paid.
Some writers called this system 'bonded labour', others
called it 'debt slavery'. What shocked Laura most was
the realisation that the amount originally borrowed
could be as little as two thousand rupees — about
thirty-seven pounds.

And alongside this poverty were the wealthy.

Laura was glad Sanjid hadn't contacted her again.
She didn't want to hear from him. The injustices that
she'd been reading about made her extremely angry. Of
course, none of it was his fault; but it was the fault of
the élite, the system, and if he was one of the élite ....

The spot between her eyes began to throb.

'Laura, it's Sanjid. Can you hear me?'

Laura closed her eyes and put her hands over her
ears to shut out the noise of the classroom.

'I've just been reading about your country,' she said
curtly, in her mind. 'There are a lot of poor people there.'

'Yes. That's why so many of us have to leave home
and work, because our parents need the money.'

'Work?' She was surprised. 'But surely you don't
work.'

'Of course I work,' giggled Sanjid.

'But I thought .... Aren't you at school in Bihar?'

'I'm not in Bihar, Laura. I'm in Mirzapur.'

'But you said you were from Bihar.'

'Bihar is my home, but it's far away. I'm in Mirzapur. I
knot carpets for my master, Babu Krishna.'

Laura felt the loneliness of the little voice inside
her head.

She couldn't make any sense of it. Sanjid, if he was

real, spoke English, so surely he was educated, and therefore ....

'Laura, I'm not rich,' said the voice in her head, 'and I've never been to school. I told you: I knot carpets, by hand, with all the other kids here.'

'But you speak English.'

'Ah!' said the voice softly. 'That's the magic. You're new to the magic, like I was with Patrice.'

'Patrice?'

'What?' said a voice in front of Laura.

She opened her eyes and looked up. Patrick Foley was staring at her from the row in front. She looked at him blankly.

'What do you want?' he said. 'You were calling me.'

'Was I? Sorry,' mumbled Laura. 'I was just thinking out loud.'

'Any time you want to tell me your dreams of me, baby,' said Patrick, grinning suggestively. 'Any time at all, you know where I am.'

'Sorry to burst your bubble,' said Laura, thinking quickly, 'but I was thinking about Patricia Cornwell, the writer.'

'Whatever, baby. The offer still stands,' laughed Patrick as he turned around.

'Yeah, right.'

Laura closed her eyes and put her hands over her face again. She would have to be more careful. She'd been talking out loud.

'Laura? Laura, are you still there?' called the voice in her head.

'I'm still here,' Laura replied. 'Who's Patrice?'

'She was the first one who came into my head. I understood everything she said, so I thought she spoke the same language as me; but she told me she lived in a place called Mozambique and spoke her own language.'

'But I understand you,' protested Laura.

'Just like I understood Patrice and I can understand Rosa, who's from a place called Brazil, and I understand you even though you're from .... Where are you, Laura?'

'Ireland.'

'I understand you, even though you're from Ireland.'

'But how?'

'I don't know how the magic works. Neither did any of the others. I just know that in the magic, we hear each other in our own languages. Do you work, Laura?'

'No,' said Laura, still trying to understand 'the magic'. 'I'm at school. But how —'

'And do you live in a house, and have a bed and a car?' asked Sanjid, ignoring her half-formed question.

'Yes, but —'

'So you're really rich?'

'No, we're not, it's ....'

Before she could finish, the voice — Sanjid — had hopped to another question.

'Laura, will you talk to Rosa? I'm worried about her. Please talk to her ....'

The voice was gone, as suddenly as it had come. Laura felt dizzy. The throbbing in her forehead had gone, but she felt slightly sick. She couldn't focus her thoughts.

'Laura! Laura?'

Sanjid's voice sounded different. It didn't seem to be coming to the normal place ....

'Laura!' said the voice again. Someone nudged Laura in the arm. She opened her eyes. Miss O'Toole, who was her class teacher as well as her religion teacher, was looking at her, smiling.

'Sorry, Miss.'

'I was just asking if you were OK. You looked miles away.'

'I'm fine, Miss. I was just thinking about something.'

'Well, now that I have everyone's full attention,' said Miss O'Toole, twirling her pigtail around her fingers, 'I have just a couple of notices. The first is ....'

chapter 7

Laura was just beginning to be able to concentrate on what Miss O'Toole was saying when Sanjid's voice broke into her thoughts again.

'Laura,' he called. 'Laura, will you talk to Rosa? Please help her.'

'I can't. Not now, Sanjid,' Laura replied, looking straight ahead at Miss O'Toole.

'But you have to!' persisted Sanjid urgently. 'She's going to do something silly. Talk to her.'

'Can't I talk to her later?'

'No. Talk to her now, please.'

'Sweet mother of God!' Laura exclaimed. 'Can't you get the idea that ....'

But he was gone. There was that void in the centre of her head again.

Laura could see Miss O'Toole's lips moving, and her eyes flicking over the notes in front of her, but she couldn't hear a word.

Then a new voice rang in her head; an angry, shouting voice.

'Hey, rich girl,' called the voice. 'I'm Rosa. Sanjid told me you want to help me.' Then the voice laughed, humourlessly.

'Sanjid asked me to talk to you,' said Laura, still looking at Miss O'Toole. 'He thinks I can help, and —'

'Help, rich bitch?' exploded Rosa. 'How are you going to help? Are you going to give me your house and your pretty clothes and your fucking fancy car, yeah? Yeah?'

'I .... Sanjid said ....' Laura was flustered.

'Sanjid's an idiot. He thinks that just because we've both got tits and periods, we've got something in common. We've got bugger-all in common, rich bitch.'

Rosa's anger was so strong that Laura had to put her head into her hands to steady herself. She was shaking.

'Tell me, rich kid, you ever looked at the kids who sleep in doorways and on the streets in your own city? Ever spoken to them?' The voice was menacing.

'No,' Laura replied quickly, nervously.

'It figures. You're like those rich bastards across town. They spit on us, off the balconies of their fancy apartments. Or they tell the big shots that we scare off the tourists and make the streets look like a mess, so they should do something about us. They give us charity at Christmas and then hire the death squads to get rid of us.'

'But I want to help,' said Laura, almost in tears. 'Sanjid said I could help.'

'Help!' Rosa laughed dismissively. 'We had help from your kind at Candelaria, and look what it did for poor Paulo and Gambazinho. Heard of Candelaria, rich kid?'

Laura didn't reply.

'I didn't think so. You haven't heard of Candelaria, and you want to *help*,' Rosa laughed. 'Find out about Candelaria, rich kid. Find out what they do to us. Look at the shit you shovel in your own streets, then talk to me about help.'

Then the voice was gone.

Laura's head was spinning. She felt breathless, but it wasn't the breathlessness of an asthma attack; it was the breathlessness of having faced pure, undiluted rage. This girl on the other side of the world didn't even know her, yet she was spewing out anger, maybe even hatred, at her. Laura had never experienced anything like it. It made her feel weak; weak, small and cowardly.

I don't need this. I really don't.

'Sorry, Laura,' said Miss O'Toole. 'Did you say something?'

Laura stood up, feeling dizzy and confused. 'Sorry, Miss. I need to get a drink. My head is killing me.'

She rushed into the toilets and held her face against the drinking taps, letting the water spurt into her eyes.

'I don't need this crap,' she said aloud. 'What the hell did I ever do to her, and what the hell's Candelaria?'

She pulled a paper towel from the dispenser, found a pencil in her blazer pocket and wrote down the word 'Candelaria'.

'Laura, Laura,' called Sanjid. 'You talked to Rosa. Isn't she lovely?'

'Lovely!' Laura said. 'That's not the word ....'

Then, involuntarily, she started to laugh. Maybe it was at Sanjid's innocence, or maybe it was just a way to release the tension caused by Rosa's tirade.

'She's wonderful,' said Laura. 'Absolutely bloody wonderful.'

'I'm glad you like her,' said Sanjid seriously. 'So glad.'

Laura tucked the paper towel into her pocket and opened the toilet door.

'Absolutely bloody wonderful,' she giggled, as she walked down the corridor.

As she made her way back to her homeroom, she could see people looking at her, staring as she spoke and laughed to herself, but what the hell. She found it funny.

chapter

8

'Candelaria,' said Mrs Taylor. 'In Brazil, you say? It sort of rings a bell.'

'I think it has something to do with death squads and street kids,' offered Laura.

The librarian shook her head. 'I wouldn't have anything on it. Are you going into town in the next few days?'

'Actually, I'm going in today.' Laura scooped the two rolls of film from Sarah's photo session out of her pocket. 'My asthma's too dodgy to use the darkroom at the moment.'

'In that case, try Amnesty. They'll probably have something, and if they don't they might tell you who will. Maybe UNICEF.'

'Thanks,' said Laura, turning to go.

'Oh, Laura,' Mrs Taylor called after her. 'I asked Marcus about Mirzapur. All he could tell me is that it's in what they call the Indian carpet belt, up around

Uttar Pradesh — remember that big province, sort of left of Bihar?'

Laura nodded.

'Apparently there's a whole area around there that produces beautiful handmade carpets. Pretty awful conditions, though, and the workers are very poorly treated — almost like slaves.'

'Slaves!'

'Yes. It's unbelievable, in this day and age, but there's this system, in a lot of India, where parents borrow money and they and their children are used as labour till the loan's repaid. Marcus said he could probably get more information if you're interested.'

'I'd appreciate that,' said Laura.

'This sounds as if it'll be a great project,' said Mrs Taylor.

'Sorry?'

'This project that you're getting all the information for. You must tell me about it sometime.'

'I will,' promised Laura. *If I ever find out myself.*

What was she getting herself into? If she was going mad, she was going mad in the most novel way she'd ever heard of — speaking to a carpet slave in India and an aggressive bitch in Brazil. Shakespeare and Ben Jonson looked very ordinary by comparison.

Slaves!

Poor bloody Sanjid.

~

The bus for town stopped a hundred yards from the school gates. On Wednesday, half-day for the fifth- and sixth-years, there was usually a crowd waiting at the bus stop; but the fifteen minutes Laura had spent in the library meant that she'd missed the rush. When she got on the bus there were only a few familiar faces. One was Gnasher's. He was sitting at the back, reading. Laura sat down beside him.

'Oh, hi,' he said, looking up from his book. Instinctively he pushed it into his pocket. Laura glanced at the title. It was John Steinbeck's *The Grapes of Wrath*.

'You're a real bloody phoney, aren't you?' she laughed.

'Me?' he said with mock innocence. 'What do you mean?'

'I mean — this yobbo act, and there you are reading Steinbeck.'

'Would you prefer me to be illiterate?'

'And you're a great pianist,' Laura went on. 'I heard you play in school, remember?'

Gnasher laughed. He'd been suspended for that: going into the music room, instead of to registration, and playing Jerry Lee Lewis's 'Whole Lotta Shakin' Goin' On' so loud that he'd almost drowned out the first-years' assembly.

'Anyway, what's your point?' he said.

'My point is,' said Laura seriously, 'why the act?'

Gnasher laughed and shook his head.

'It's not an act. What you see is what you get. I like Steinbeck. The thing about writers like him is that they tell the truth. They talk about the way ordinary people get screwed over by the money-men and their hired thugs — the way money takes over society, and humanity goes out the window. I believe that, and .... Oh, balls!' He looked out of the window and nodded. 'And just when things were getting going.'

Laura followed his gaze. Sarah was standing at the bus stop. She'd already changed out of her uniform; she looked ready for a 'Miss Teen Fashion' competition.

'Do me a favour, Laura,' said Gnasher earnestly. 'Keep that bitch as far away from me as possible. She really gets on my tits, the brain-dead prat.'

'But I was just getting interested in Dr Coyle's philosophy of life. I want to know where all this insight came from.'

'From what happened to my dad and my granddad,' Gnasher said quickly, keeping one eye on Sarah. 'I promise I'll tell you all about it sometime, but please — I would consider it a great act of personal kindness ....'

Laura got up and moved to a seat three rows in front. 'You owe me one,' she whispered to him.

As she settled into the seat, she suddenly realised that, in all the years she'd known Gnasher, that was as close as she'd ever got to having a real conversation with him.

'Oh, hi,' said Sarah, sitting down beside Laura un-invited. 'I was looking for you earlier on. I was wondering if you had the photos ready yet. I'm hoping to sent the portfolio in to an agency next week.'

Laura reached into her pocket and took out the two rolls of film. 'Here's the photo shoot,' she said. 'I'm leaving them in to the processors.'

'Is it the same one you always use, the one in Abbey Street?'

Laura nodded.

'I'm going that way, to have a look in the shops in the Jervis Centre. We can go together.'

Not if I can help it.

'Listen, maybe you could take them. I have to go to Amnesty and UNICEF, and they're in the other direction.'

'Saving the world again?' smiled Sarah.

'Yeah, something like that.' Laura put the film into Sarah's hand.

'But won't they want a deposit or something?'

'Probably about a fiver.'

'But I haven't got enough money,' protested Sarah.

Laura put her hand into the breast pocket of her

blazer and pulled out a five-pound note. She handed it to Sarah without speaking.

'So, how's it going?' asked Sarah.

'What?'

'Things in general. We haven't seen much of each other this week.'

'You wouldn't want to know,' replied Laura, wondering how Sarah could have forgotten their little exchange at registration.

She turned her head towards the window. Gnasher smiled and gave her the thumbs-up.

Jesus, what a turnaround. I'd rather be back there with him than up here with Superbitch.

She giggled to find herself thinking the nickname.

'What?' asked Sarah.

'Sorry. Just thinking about something. It's not important.'

'Jesus, Laura, you're really going weird,' said Sarah patronizingly. 'Some strange things going on in your head.'

'You don't know the half of it.'

Laura spent the rest of the journey looking out of the window, occasionally nodding politely and putting in the odd 'yes' or 'I see,' as Sarah kept up a running monologue. At times she felt mean, because she just wanted Sarah to go away. At other times she felt guilty, because Sarah was genuinely being friendly. But then she reminded herself of what she'd overheard in the toilets. That was how genuine Sarah was. It didn't matter what she said. Things would never be the same again.

~

'How long will you be in wherever you're going?' Sarah asked as they got off the bus.

'Don't know. Half an hour, maybe three-quarters.'

'I won't be much longer myself. How about meeting

in Bewley's in about an hour?'

'I'll probably go for a coffee. If I'm there, I'm there.'
Laura turned and walked away.

'OK,' Sarah called after her.

'You know, I'll never know what you saw in her,'
said Gnasher, running to catch up with Laura. 'Or the
other two — Cass and Tina, right?'

'We were friends for years.'

'Yeah, but you've had absolutely nothing in common
with them for ages. It's been obvious — to me, at least.'

'Really?'

'Yeah. You've become Laura the radical, and they've
just become dedicated followers of fashion — and, in
her case, a real bitch. You know what I reckon?'

'No, but you're going to tell me,' said Laura, stop-
ping at the door to the Amnesty shop.

'I don't reckon it was friendship. I reckon it was
habit. They were that favourite teddy bear you'd out-
grown but didn't want to put away.'

'You're some psychologist.'

'I thought I was a phoney?'

'That too, definitely.'

Gnasher held the door to the Amnesty shop open
and walked in after Laura.

'You coming in too?' she asked.

Before he could reply, one of the girls behind the
counter threw a key to him.

'Dave, catch!'

He caught the key and turned to the door marked
'Staff only'.

'I'm here every Wednesday,' he said, turning the key
in the lock. 'Volunteer. See ya.'

He disappeared through the door.

That guy is one surprise after another, Laura thought.

chapter
9

Laura sipped her cappuccino as she flicked through the report on Candelaria. She wasn't really reading it; she was just picking out the odd phrase here and there. She'd read it later.

'Any good jokes in that?' asked Sarah, sitting down opposite her with a Coke and a doughnut.

Laura smiled. 'Actually, no.' She slipped the report back into her bag. She really didn't want to talk to Sarah, but she wasn't going to be rude.

'Well, aren't you going to ask me what I bought?' demanded Sarah, digging into her bags.

Laura didn't reply. She didn't need to. Sarah was going to show her anyway.

'Look at this,' said Sarah, holding up a hanger draped with a tiny bra-and-knickers set, red lace with black frills. 'It's La Perla! It was on sale — only thirty-five quid. What do you think?'

Laura was saved from replying: in a sudden flurry of

activity, Sarah quickly pushed the set back into her bag.

'Oh, quick, let's pretend to laugh,' she said, laughing. She was looking directly over Laura's shoulder.

Laura turned around. Conor was coming towards them, checking his hair in each wall mirror he passed. Laura quickly finished her coffee and stood up.

'Going already?' asked Conor.

'Very perceptive of you,' said Laura.

'I'll come with you ... sweet thing.'

Sweet thing? This dickhead has definitely watched one film too many.

Conor put his arm around Laura and tried to peck her on the cheek. Laura pushed him away.

'It wouldn't be very gallant of you to come with me while Sarah's still eating. I'm sure she'd appreciate the company.'

She turned and walked out without waiting to hear his reply.

They deserve each other. They really do. Egos of the world unite.

~

'You have to be cold, look right in their eyes, kill them and smile at them. I've always done it like that.'

Laura felt her stomach lurch. It had nothing to do with the movement of the bus.

It was what she was reading.

Mario Peiriama de Andrade was twenty years old when he was sentenced to life imprisonment for killing street children in Brazil. Amnesty International had reproduced part of an interview with him in their brochure 'Death Squads in South America'. The interview had been part of a *World In Action* TV programme on street kids in Rio de Janeiro.

Laura read his words again. 'Bastard,' she whispered

under her breath. 'Heartless, murdering bastard.'

A few seconds later she was repeating the words to describe the unknown murderer of nine-year-old Patricio da Silva. (*Nine! That's the same age as Katie is next month.*) Patricio's body had been found on the roadside in Ipanema, a suburb of Rio. His murderer had left a note 'justifying' his or her actions hanging around the child's neck.

'I killed you,' it said, 'because you didn't study and had no future. The government must not allow the city to be invaded by kids.'

Rosa was right. I don't have any idea what her life's like.

Seven million kids had to fend for themselves on the streets of Brazil. Laura couldn't even comprehend the figure. The biggest crowds she'd ever seen had been in the video of the 1994 World Cup Final, and those had been only fifty or sixty thousand people at most.

Seven million! That's twice the entire population of Ireland. Seven million, and all kids!

And all at risk from the death squads.

Was that really Rosa's life?

Laura shivered involuntarily. She really didn't have any idea, did she? She hadn't even seen a street kid.

No, that wasn't true. She'd seen Dublin street kids, but there weren't seven million of them — Laura wasn't sure what the number was, but she'd never seen more than a handful. She'd always felt frightened or intimidated by them. She'd heard some were shoplifters and pickpockets. That was probably true: with no homes, no money, and no other way to survive, of course some of them would be dragged into crime. But then again, some of the kids in Laura's school were shoplifters, and some had been caught breaking into houses; and they came from nice, secure, middle-class homes ....

But no matter how irritating or intimidating she found the street kids in Dublin, she couldn't imagine death squads roaming around killing them. Nor could she imagine an Irish equivalent of Mario Peiriama de Andrade saying that he thought no more of killing street kids then he would of killing flies, because they were thieves and vermin.

The Irish would never let that happen, would they?

~

Captain's Log
Wednesday, 25 October
10.35 p.m.

Jesus! What a day. Now I've got a head-pal in Brazil. She's an aggressive bitch, but after what I've been reading, I can see why. I can't believe all this stuff about death squads. It's unreal. There's a whole world out there I have no idea about.

Captain's Log (Supplemental)
Wednesday, 25 October
11.45 p.m.

Rosa says I haven't a clue. She's right, but I've just thought of something that might help me get some in-sight. Maybe after tonight I'll have _some_ idea.

chapter
10

Laura tiptoed softly downstairs. She was wearing her combats, boots, two sweatshirts, and a combat jacket. Under her arm she carried a thin tartan blanket.

I have to know.

She turned off the burglar alarm and quietly opened the back door. It was 2.15 in the morning and the estate was fairly quiet, only the sound of the occasional car breaking the stillness. Laura laid the blanket on the ground and shivered in the early-morning air. She had only been outside for a few minutes, and she was already cold.

She lay on the blanket, pulling the corners tightly around her. Tonight she'd be one of sixty million kids in the world — maybe even a hundred million; no one seemed to know the real figure — sleeping rough. But it was different for her; she knew that. She had an alternative. Any time she felt like it, she could change her mind and go back inside, into the warmth of the house and the comfort and security of her own bed. Few of the others had that option. For one reason or another, the streets were the only home they had.

And she would be safe. She would be lying in the security of her own back garden, in a nice middle-class suburb. If she decided to stay outside, she could sleep without fear of being attacked by other street kids, criminal gangs, vigilantes, or death squads.

She looked up at the stars. How many of the other kids sleeping under those stars wouldn't live to see the morning? How many would share the fate of the kids at Candelaria?

Laura didn't know much about Brazil. She knew it was in South America and was famous for coffee, footballers and the Copacabana Beach. She also knew it was a very poor country, although some of its residents were extremely wealthy. But that was all she had known, until that day. She'd never heard of Candelaria before Rosa mentioned it. Now that she knew, she could understand the anger and pure unbridled aggression that Rosa felt towards people like her. Candelaria was beyond belief.

On 23 July 1993, a gang of hooded men opened fire on a group of over fifty street children who were sleeping rough near the Candelaria church, one of the most prominent landmarks in Rio de Janeiro. Seven children and one young adult were killed.

Four boys died instantly; a fifth was killed as he ran away. Three others were abducted in a car. Two of them were shot dead in the nearby Aterro do Flamengo Gardens. The other died of his wounds four days later. Another young adult, Wagner dos Santos, was also abducted to Aterro do Flamengo Gardens, where he was shot in the face and left for dead. But he survived the shooting.

Shortly after the massacre, three military police officers and one civilian were charged with the murders. Later, five more men were implicated in the massacre.

On 30 April 1996, Marcos Vinicius Borges Emanuel, a twenty-nine-year-old military policeman, faced trial on charges relating to the Candelaria murders. The following day he was sentenced to 309 years' imprisonment for his part in the killings. In June 1996, a second trial reduced the sentence to eighty-nine years. Under Brazilian law he will be subject to a maximum prison term of thirty years.

The trial of the three other men indicted in 1993 — two military policemen and one civilian — was postponed. They were all released on 14 May 1996 pending trial.

Three more military policemen were also detained in connection with the massacre, and a fourth came forward to confess his part in the killings.

Laura shivered again, but not with cold this time. When the report had been written, in July 1996, none of those seven men charged with being involved in the massacre had been brought to trial. She didn't know if that had changed since, but the thought that they could still be at large frightened her. What was to stop them killing the other witnesses?

She turned over on her side and looked at the wall.

What if I was one of those survivors? What if I had seen the massacre? How would I feel now, knowing those others were still out there — maybe ready to come and get me to make sure I couldn't say anything?

She could see it clearly. Men crawling over the wall — men with machine-guns at their sides and pistols in their hands. They came over the wall, creeping low across the grass, calling to her.

'Laura, little Laura, we've come for you. We're here, Laura ....'

Laura felt her legs and arms begin to tremble.

I can't do this, she told herself firmly, turning onto her back and concentrating on the stars. *If I get too scared, I'll give up and go back to bed, and I can't do that. I have to know what it's like to sleep rough, to have these feelings. I can't give in.*

But she couldn't stop the fear.

Is this how Wagner dos Santos felt?

He'd survived being shot in the face and left for dead in Aterro do Flamengo Gardens, and he'd come forward as a witness to the massacre. Then, in December 1994, while under State protection, he had been abducted and shot again. Again he had survived, although the attack had left his face partially paralysed. It was believed that those responsible for the second attempt on his life were also members of Rio de Janeiro's military police force.

He was believed to be in safe custody outside Brazil.

Was this how he spent his nights, waiting for them to come? And the other witnesses to the massacre, those who were too frightened to testify — did they wait too? Did they lie awake listening for strange sounds or unfamiliar voices, too frightened to sleep in case someone came for them, to make sure that they couldn't change their minds?

Laura pulled the blanket closer around her. *Jesus, I'm freezing.* The temperature was dropping. She could feel the cold creeping into every part of her body.

This was what it was like for the other street kids. Even those who didn't have to worry about death squads still had to fight the cold.

When she'd arrived home from town she'd asked her mother about street kids in Dublin. Working in a refuge for battered wives, Chris Byrne came across all sorts of facts and statistics.

'According to Focus Point, there are nearly five hundred homeless kids in Dublin. Of course, that doesn't mean they're all on the streets, but some of them are. And I was talking to an English researcher who reckoned that Ireland had more street kids than any other country in Europe.'

'I find that hard to believe, Chris,' Joe interrupted. 'I mean, since the fall of the old Soviet bloc there are thousands of kids sleeping in railway stations and bus shelters in places like Russia and Romania. I can't believe we're worse than that.'

'Well, that's what she said, Joe,' answered Chris. 'I find it hard to believe as well, but apparently there's some centre at Trinity College that has all the details. Maybe you should get some info from them, Laura.'

'Why bother?' said Kev, picking up half of the conversation as he passed through the kitchen to get his Gameboy.

'Chris, are you sure you brought the right baby home from hospital?' asked Joe, pointing to Kev's disappearing back. 'Sometimes I can't believe he's ours.'

'Maybe he's a robot from the planet Tron,' offered Katie seriously.

Or a dickhead from the planet Asshole, thought Laura, as she replayed the scene in her mind.

She closed her eyes.

~

'Laura — Laura! For Christ's sake, Laura, wake up!'

Laura could hear the panic in the voice and feel the hands shaking her urgently. She opened her eyes. Kev was leaning over her, looking at her anxiously.

'Thank fuck for that!' he said with relief. 'I thought you were dead.'

There were real tears welling up in his eyes.

'I'm OK. I just wanted —'

'You just want to be put in the nut-house!' Kev said, offering her his hand as he stood up.

Laura reached out and grabbed his hand. She was freezing and damp with dew, and every part of her body ached. She climbed onto one knee and pushed herself up, painfully.

'What time is it?'

'It's half-six,' Kev said. 'I got up to watch the repeat of yesterday's episode of *The X-Men*, it's on in fifteen minutes. I was just making myself a cup of coffee when I looked out and saw you.'

They went into the kitchen and Kev handed Laura a cup of coffee. Laura wrapped her hands around the cup. The heat almost made her cry.

'You nearly gave me a heart attack, you fucking idiot.' Kev took off his dressing-gown and put it around Laura's shoulders. Then he took her duffel coat from the back of the door and put that around her too. 'You're freezing, you prat. What were you doing out there, anyway?'

Laura didn't answer; she just pulled the coat tightly around her. 'Thanks,' she said hoarsely.

Kev didn't pursue the question.

'You'd better go up, before Mom and Dad come down and see you like that. You look like shit.' He opened the kitchen door and pointed to the stairs.

Laura smiled.

Maybe he's not such an uncaring dickhead after all.

'You're a real fucking idiot,' Kev said firmly, as Laura made her way up the stairs. She heard the little catch in his voice as he added, almost to himself, 'You could have frozen to death out there, you prat.'

Maybe not a dickhead at all.

She put the coffee cup on her locker. Katie rolled

over in her sleep, smiled and said something that sounded like 'goal'. Laura pulled back the duvet, took off her coat and Kev's dressing-gown and climbed into bed fully dressed, boots and all.

How many didn't make it to morning? she wondered as her head hit the pillow. *How many froze to death? How many met friends of Mr Andrade?*

chapter
11

'I was just really cold, so I got up and got dressed,' Laura fibbed.

Her mother looked at her. 'Boots and all?' she said incredulously.

'I was ... I was sort of half-asleep, and I ....'

Chris checked her watch and placed a hand on Laura's forehead.

'It's eight o'clock. I want you to get undressed and get back into bed. I'll check you again in about twenty minutes, and if you're still this hot, you can spend the rest of the day in there.'

Laura rolled out of bed and started to undress.

'Really, Lar, sometimes I think Katie's got more sense than you. You know getting a temperature could set your asthma off.'

Laura stripped down to her pants, grabbed her 'Save the Whale' T-shirt off the floor, pulled it over her head and jumped back into bed.

She hated lying to her mother, but she couldn't think of what else to say. Somehow, 'I was cold so I got up and got dressed' seemed a little more acceptable than 'I spent the night sleeping in the garden to see what it's like to be a street kid.'

She put her hand under her pillow, pulled out her diary and pen and started writing.

Captain's Log
Thursday, 26 October
8.10 a.m.

Rosa's right: I don't have a clue.

It doesn't matter how cold I was out there — it wasn't real, was it? It was just playing at being a street kid. I mean, I knew I could get up and walk away any time I wanted to. If I got too cold or too scared I just had to walk back in here and climb into my nice warm bed.

I've absolutely no idea what it's like for someone who doesn't have that option.

Maybe it's easier for them. Maybe if you're born into that way of life you get used to it; or maybe if you start sleeping rough young enough, or if you're tougher than I am, then it's easier — especially if you don't have any alternatives to think about.

Jesus! What a load of middle-class twaddle that is!

'Oh, it's easy for them, dear, they're used to it. They're different from us, they don't feel pain the way we do. And anyway, we don't have homeless people here. It's only in those nasty Third World countries.'

Well, we do. And it's not right. People shouldn't have to live like this.

But at least here we don't have death squads — yet.

Christ, I was frightened enough just imagining someone coming over the wall to get me. What must it be like for real? I couldn't handle that at all. I'd just run, run as fast and as far as I could — either that or I'd die of fright.

Rosa's right. I don't have a clue.

She sounded as if she knew all about Candelaria. If that's true, she's in real danger.

Why doesn't she get out? Why doesn't she just run?

Laura snapped her diary closed and shoved it under her pillow.

'Rosa, Rosa,' she called silently, putting her hands over her face and closing her eyes tightly. 'Rosa, it's Laura. I found out about Candelaria. Can you hear me? Rosa, talk to me. I tried to find out what it's like, but I can't. Rosa, I want to know.'

Laura felt a throbbing in the centre of her forehead.

'Hey, it's the spoilt brat,' giggled the voice inside her head. 'So you tried to find out what it's like. What'd ya do, put milk in your coffee instead of cream?'

'I —'

'You wanna know what it's like?' Rosa demanded, cutting Laura off. Her voice was slurred. For a moment it trailed off into a mumble; then it was back again, angry, commanding. 'You wanna know what it's like? Close your eyes. I'll show you!'

Laura closed her eyes.

'Look, rich bitch. Welcome to my world.'

Laura felt a sudden intense pain in the centre of her head. She tightened her eyes and rubbed her forehead, trying to ease the pain. A brilliant blue light poured into the spot between her eyes. Through the light she saw images, figures, flickering and moving.

~

Four young boys, naked from the waist up, sprawled on old abandoned car seats in front of a small bonfire, swaying and giggling, chattering in a language Laura couldn't understand. That was strange: if she could understand Rosa, why couldn't she understand them? Maybe the magic only worked when she was addressed directly?

As the image sharpened, Laura could see that two of the boys had dark skin and dark wavy hair. A third was black and wore his hair in small knots. The fourth was dark-skinned but, strangely, had bright red hair in an Afro. He was turned slightly to the side, and he held a plastic bag tightly against his face.

The images were so clear that Laura might have been watching television, but television wouldn't have brought her the stench of stale urine and excrement that assaulted her nostrils, or the deafening sound of traffic that seemed to come from every side.

She was there!

She was seeing through Rosa's eyes, hearing through Rosa's ears, experiencing the same smells, feeling the same movements as Rosa. It was as if they'd somehow merged into one person, even though Laura knew she was still at home in her own bed. The realisation both frightened and excited her.

'How —' she began, bewildered.

'Magic,' laughed Rosa, tauntingly. 'Magic. This is my world. Enjoy it.'

The images swayed slightly, as if someone was shaking the camera, or as if the viewer was drunk.

Drunk!

'Not yet, rich brat, but soon,' giggled Rosa. 'Soon.'

The red-haired boy lifted a bottle from his side and drank from it long and hard. He looked older than the others, maybe fifteen. The others didn't look any older than Katie.

'Me next, Gilberto!' called Rosa.

The angle of the image changed. The camera moved slowly, unsteadily, making its way around the fire.

As Rosa moved, Laura glimpsed traffic moving on a small road not far away, and saw the ugly concrete arches of a flyover rising above her. They were sitting under a highway. A thin mongrel dog scampered between the four boys and a group of other kids who were sitting closer to the edge of the road. A baby about eighteen months old was sitting in the dirt, playing with a tin can. Apart from a small, grubby vest, it was naked. As it pushed itself up, raising its bottom in the air, Laura could see that its bare bottom and legs were filthy.

This must be a dream, she told herself.

'Oh, it's not a dream!' giggled Rosa, drunkenly. 'But if you want dreams, look — here's where to find them ....'

Chubby brown hands stretched out towards Gilberto. He turned and tried to move, but the hands grabbed the plastic bag away from his mouth and nose. The plastic bag came towards Laura's face — Rosa's face. She could see the brown gooey liquid in the bottom.

Glue.

'No!' Laura yelled. 'No!'

The bag covered her eyes, her nose and mouth — Rosa's nose and mouth. She heard the deep breathing.

~

Laura's eyes were burning. Her head was spinning. As the warm, sickly smell reached her lungs, she felt her chest tighten so hard that she thought her ribs would crush her heart. She couldn't breathe. She tried to drag air into her lungs, but nothing would come.

She snapped her eyes open, gasped for air and turned frantically to her bedside locker, fumbling for her inhaler. She forced it into her mouth and pumped it once, twice, three times. The spray hit the back of her throat and for a second her throat opened, allowing a gulp of air to enter her lungs. Then it closed again.

Laura panicked. She felt as if the thick brown goo had sealed her throat and nose shut. She rocked back and forward, trying to force herself to breathe. Another little gasp entered her lungs; then they seemed to close again, blocking out air just as the shutter of a camera blocks out the light.

'Well, Lar, let's see how you're doing,' smiled her mother, pushing the bedroom door open. 'You ....'

Laura looked at her, pleading with her eyes for help.

'*Lar!*' Chris rushed to the bed, screaming over her shoulder, 'Quick, Joe, call an ambulance! She can't breathe!'

Laura heard her father dialling 999. Chris put her arms around her, half-dragged, half-lifted her from the bed, and pulled her towards the open window.

'Pant, Lar,' she ordered, as she pulled back the curtain and forced Laura's head into the morning air. 'Pant.'

Laura tried to pant, but nothing would come.

'Try, Lar. Try and pant,' pleaded Chris.

Laura felt as if her head and chest were ready to explode. Her knees began to buckle under her. Things were growing darker. She felt her mother gently lowering her to the bed, forcing her mouth open. She felt their lips touch. Something sweet and cool poured into her mouth ....

chapter
12

Laura was the only patient in the ward. The others were in the day room, watching television. She lay on the bed, staring at the ceiling, waiting for Dr Heffernan to come and tell her she could go home. She was fully dressed and her bag was packed and lying on the floor.

As soon as she'd woken to find the oxygen tubes taped to her nose and the drip attached to her arm, she'd known the attack had been severe. But she hadn't realised that it could have been fatal until she'd overheard the whispered conversation between her mother and the doctor, the previous night.

That lousy bitch, Rosa!

Laura concentrated on the tiny holes in the ceiling tiles, trying to block out the name. She just wanted to get home and forget about everything that had happened: the attack, Rosa, Sanjid — everything.

They nearly killed me! I nearly died because of them, and I'm damned if that's going to happen again. They can go to hell.

But they wouldn't leave her alone.

They'd been calling to her almost non-stop, day and night, for the five days she'd been in the hospital. But she wouldn't reply. She just concentrated on a space between her eyes and filled her mind with any thoughts that would block out Sanjid and Rosa. And every time she blocked them, their voices grew weaker. Pretty soon she wouldn't be able to hear them at all. *Thank God.*

Why was she even bothering to think about them?

She turned onto her side and looked at the cards on her bedside locker. There were five of them: one from her mom and dad, one from Kev, a home-made one from Katie, one from Miss O'Toole, and — the real surprise — one from Gnasher and Kelz. *That boy never ceases to amaze me*, Laura thought. His message was a bit cryptic — 'Fight the good fight!' — but at least he'd thought of her.

The girls hadn't bothered to send a card. They hadn't phoned, they hadn't called in — even though the hospital was only a fifteen-minute bus ride from where they all lived — and, as far as Laura knew, they hadn't even asked about her. Kev admitted that, when she pushed him on it. That hurt. It left a huge, stinging, hollow feeling in her stomach.

~

'Laura? Laura, I know you can hear me. Please answer me, Laura, please,' called the voice inside her head. Rosa.

Laura closed her eyes and concentrated on blocking her out. 'Before 1500, the Catholic Church was the majority church all over Europe, but over the next hundred years its power declined. Many countries broke away from the authority of Rome. This period is called the Reformation ....'

She stopped.

'Laura — Laura! I know you can hear me! For fuck's sake, answer me. Please!'

'There were a number of causes of the Reformation, but chief among them were the abuses in the Church. The major abuses were simony, nepotism, pluralism, absenteeism and the sale of indulgences —'

'Laura, I'm sorry. I'm really, really sorry. Please don't cut me off. Please don't be so cruel, Laura.'

'Simony was the practise of selling positions of authority in the Church. Nepotism was the appointment of relatives to positions within the Church for which they were not qualified ....'

Laura stopped. The voice had gone.

She sighed and rolled over onto her side.

She was almost beyond their reach. Soon they'd be gone for ever.

Cruel!

The word seemed to explode in her head.

Cruel! Did that selfish little bitch accuse me of being cruel? That's bloody great. She nearly kills me, and I'm the one who's being cruel.

Laura pushed herself off the bed and paced around the room. The word acted like a key opening the door to some place where four days of fear and anger had been locked up. Suddenly she was shaking with rage.

Who does that stupid bitch think she is? I'm the one who nearly died, not her. Her bloody glue-sniffing nearly killed me, and now she's calling me cruel because I won't answer her! She can piss off!

She clenched her fists and punched the nearest bed as hard as she could.

She's the last person in the world I'd want to speak to — her and that stupid little prat, Sanjid! It was his fault I made contact with her in the first place. Him and his bloody whining — 'Help her, oh, please, Laura, help her ....' Well, I tried to help her and look where it got me. They can drop dead, both of them. Rosa needs something, all right, but it's not help. She needs a good smack, right across her stupid, ugly mouth.

Laura wanted to pick something up and smash it against the wall, or tear the bedclothes to shreds, or throw a chair through the window. Instead, she threw herself angrily into an armchair and thumped the arms with her clenched fists.

She had no right to do that to me! It's not my fault that she has to live like that. I didn't make the kids sleep on the streets! I didn't send the death squads into Candelaria! I didn't do anything to her. So who the hell does she think she is, taking it out on me? She has no right. No right at all. I only wanted to help.

Laura fell back into the chair, exhausted.

God, she hated getting angry. She couldn't handle it, all that shouting and screaming and 'letting it all out'. Kev was brilliant at it. If anyone crossed him, he'd rant and rave and scream at them from now to next Friday; and then he'd just walk away, quite happy. It wouldn't cost him a thought, and if the other person didn't like it — tough! The strange thing was that, nine times out of ten, the person he'd been ranting at would come crawling back with an apology. When that happened, Kev would either just say 'It's OK, forget it,' or tell them to fuck off and never speak to them again. Either way, it didn't bother him.

Laura wished she could be like that, but she couldn't. If someone hurt her, she'd just walk away, withdraw behind an invisible wall and cut herself off. And later, when she did explode, it wouldn't be to them. It'd be to herself. After that, she'd either ignore them completely or treat them with polite indifference.

That was what she'd done with the girls, and that was what she was doing with Rosa.

As her anger gave way to exhaustion, regret and guilt began to creep in. That was what always happened, even when she knew she was in the right.

So Rosa had nearly killed her with that bloody glue-sniffing; but she hadn't meant to, had she? It had been an accident. She didn't know Laura was an asthmatic, and the poor sod probably didn't even know the dangers of glue-sniffing. Sure, it had been mean and nasty of her; but then, that was pretty much the way life was for Rosa: mean and nasty.

Laura shivered, remembering the cold terror that she'd felt in the back garden. If she had to live like that all the time, maybe she'd be like Rosa. Who was she to judge?

And poor old Sanjid. Why was she angry with him? He hadn't done anything. He'd just wanted her to help a friend, and now she was ignoring him too. That wasn't fair ....

'No!' hissed Laura angrily, banging her arms against the sides of the chair, as the guilt and sympathy gave way to anger again. 'No! Screw them! There's no excuse for what she did to me, no matter how hard life is. So screw the pair of them. They can just piss off and leave me alone.'

'I hope that's not me you're giving out about.'

Laura looked up. Dr Heffernan was leaning against the door-frame, smiling at her.

Oh, God! How long has he been there?

'I hope I don't make you feel like that,' he said. He removed the clipboard from the bottom of Laura's bed and lowered himself into a chair beside her.

Laura shook her head.

'It's good to get angry, sometimes,' Dr Heffernan

said. 'Particularly if someone's been making you do something you don't really want to do.'

He lowered his voice.

'Just between you and me, I've been meaning to ask you: *was* it just letting yourself get too hot that brought on the attack, or was it something else?'

Laura wasn't surprised. She'd been waiting for that question ever since she'd woken up in the hospital bed to find Dr Heffernan smiling down at her. She'd sensed right away that he didn't believe what he'd been told. It wasn't anything he'd said. It was more his tone and body language — the way he'd smile a little nervously, raise one eyebrow and, almost imperceptibly, shrug his shoulders. It was as if he wanted to say something else but couldn't figure out how to do it discreetly.

He was at it again.

'I can assure you of total doctor-patient confidentiality,' he continued, when Laura didn't answer. 'No one else will know.'

Laura smiled. His 'professional' act didn't really suit him. He couldn't have been that much older than she was; when he tried to sound fatherly, it just made her want to laugh.

'There's no more to it than you've already been told,' she said, leaning back in the chair. 'I didn't do anything wrong, or take anything, if that's what you're thinking.'

For a second, now that she'd actually given voice to his suspicions, the doctor looked flustered.

'I'm not implying — I mean, I'm not saying .... It's just ....'

He stopped and looked at his notes to compose himself.

'Look, Laura, I'll level with you. It hasn't been that long since I was seventeen, and I know the pressures that can be put on kids of your age.'

'Do you, Father Time?' Laura laughed, forcing him to smile and relax.

'Oh, hell, I'm not very good at this. But you are telling me the truth, aren't you? I'm asking now as a friend.' Dr Heffernan's tone and manner had switched again. 'There wasn't any more to it than what you've already told me, was there?'

'I swear,' said Laura seriously, looking straight into his eyes, 'I've never, ever taken any drugs. That is the one-hundred-percent God-given truth.'

For a moment there was silence between them.

He's looking for some sign that I'm lying.

He wouldn't find any. She mightn't have told anyone the full story, but she wasn't lying.

'I do believe you, you know,' he said finally. 'It's just — well, when you were brought in, I thought .... There was a kind of ....' He shook his head and let the sentence trail off, unfinished. 'And just now you seemed to be pretty mad at someone. I just thought .... Oh, it doesn't matter. I really do believe you.'

Laura wondered what he'd been going to say. Maybe he'd smelt something when she'd been brought in. She'd heard that the odour of glue could stay on your breath for days. Or maybe he'd noticed burns; little burn marks around the lips, mouth and throat were another sign of glue-sniffing. Laura didn't see how any of that could have been possible in her case. But she didn't ask. She didn't want to prolong the conversation. She just wanted to forget the whole experience.

Dr Heffernan scribbled something in his notes.

'Well, I've already told your mother, but since you're nearly eighteen, I'll tell you as well. You know that attack was very severe?'

Laura nodded, dreading what was coming next.

'But the good news is, you haven't done any permanent damage.'

'*Yes!*' Laura was so relieved that she almost screamed with delight. She hadn't really thought there would be any permanent damage; but there'd still been a tiny, niggling doubt at the back of her mind that something could have happened to her heart or lungs. That wasn't unknown with glue-sniffing. But she was fine. She'd been given the all-clear.

'Nope!' Dr Heffernan continued, smiling. 'You've got a heart like an ox and lungs like a gorilla.'

'Very flattering,' said Laura, smiling.

'And the even better news,' he continued, 'is that unless you rush off and become a chain-smoker or anything like that —'

'Not a chance!'

'Good. Well, provided you don't, and provided you don't do anything else stupid, there's absolutely no reason you should ever experience anything like that again.' He pushed himself out of the chair.

'If I do, I'll give you a shout,' Laura laughed.

'Well, you'll have to have a very loud voice.' Dr Heffernan replaced the clipboard on the end of her bed. 'Because I'm off. In six weeks I'm flying the coop — it'll be bye-bye Saint Peter's, hello beautiful downtown Kathmandu.'

'Kathmandu?' said Laura, surprised. 'I thought that was one of those makey-uppy places, like Jibberovia or Ballygobackwards.'

'Ah, the ignorance of modern youth. Don't they teach you anything at school these days? Kathmandu, young lady, is the capital of Nepal, which is ....'

'Just above Bihar State in India,' said Laura, recalling the map Mrs Taylor had shown her.

'I'm impressed, very impressed. Anyway, that's where I'm off to, for two years as a medical volunteer.'

'Now it's my turn to be impressed,' said Laura.

The pager on Dr Heffernan's white coat began emitting a high-pitched beep.

'Gotta go,' he said, patting Laura on the head as if she were a little girl. 'Be good, and don't do anything silly.'

'I won't,' called Laura, watching the white coat disappear through the ward door. 'Don't worry.'

She was going home. She'd been given the all-clear. She had absolutely nothing to worry about.

Then the guilt kicked in again.

chapter
13

The cycle of guilt and anger continued all day. Laura couldn't shake it. Her conversation on the journey home consisted mainly of yes-or-no answers to whatever questions she was asked, and she didn't say much more as she sat through the welcome-home tea Katie had prepared for her. She couldn't help it. For the first time, she really understood what people meant when they said something was 'wrecking my head' or 'tearing me apart'.

But her resolve hadn't weakened. She was going to continue to block Sanjid and Rosa until they left her alone. She had to. She couldn't take the risk of exposing herself to them again. Rosa's anger, stupidity, and ignorance had nearly killed her.

What if next time there was no 'nearly' about it?

Much as she felt sorry for Rosa and wanted to help her, Laura had to protect herself. And she couldn't continue to communicate with Sanjid either. He'd put her into that situation, even if he'd done it unwittingly; what if he did it again? She had to ignore him, for her own safety.

Laura wouldn't forget them. She knew that. She would never forget what she had seen and felt, but she had to leave it. She had to let it go wherever things go when they're no longer the main thing on your mind — like the pictures of starving babies in Rwanda, or the story of the old Serb woman who used a sharpened spoon to gouge out the eyes of her Muslim neighbours. Those images had haunted Laura for days, never leaving her alone for a minute, no matter what she was doing. Then, one day, they'd just slipped away. They hadn't been forgotten, but they only slipped out now and again, and when they did they never seemed quite as powerful and threatening as they once had.

That was what would happen to Sanjid and Rosa. They wouldn't be forgotten; they just wouldn't be remembered as often.

Laura rolled over, listening in the dark as Katie softly mumbled in her sleep. She closed her eyes and slowly began to drift away into a calm, soothing sleep.

~

'Laura, it's Rosa. Talk to me. Please, I'm begging you.'

Laura was almost asleep. 'Oh, push off and leave me alone,' she mumbled drowsily.

Then she realised her mistake. Suddenly she was wide awake.

'What?' she snapped angrily. 'What?'

'Oh, thank you for answering,' Rosa replied softly. 'I thought you were never going to speak to me again.'

'I'm not! You nearly killed me.'

'I know,' said Rosa. 'I'm sorry. I didn't mean to!'

'Oh, well! That makes everything all right, then,

doesn't it?' replied Laura sarcastically. 'That would have looked great on my gravestone. "Killed — but not on purpose." Dead is still fucking dead, you know!'

'I know. If you never wanted to speak to me again, I'd understand. I just wanted to say sorr —'

'You'd understand!' Laura said angrily. 'Well, isn't that bloody big of you!'

Rosa didn't reply, but Laura knew she was still there. She could sense her. The link hadn't been broken.

'Oh, for fuck's sake, say something.'

'I thought you didn't want to speak to me,' Rosa replied, almost timidly.

'I don't — but I'm still here, aren't I? So say something.'

'I'm really very sorr —'

'You've already said that,' said Laura sharply. 'What I want to know is, what gave you the right to do it? I only wanted to talk to you, to see if I could help you.'

'I know. I had no right. I was stupid, stupid and mean.' Rosa stopped, then added quickly, apologetically, 'I was drunk, you know.'

'Of course I know,' replied Laura, still angry. 'But you could have killed me — and yourself.'

'I'm sorry about you. But me — well, it's just a matter of time. It doesn't matter.'

'Oh, don't be so stupid! Of course you matter. You're too young to die by playing with all that crap!'

'Laura, what fucking difference does it make how I die? I'm dead anyway — we all are, everyone you saw that night. It's just a matter of when and where.'

Laura felt herself go cold with fear. She knew what Rosa was talking about.

'Candelaria.' She said it as a statement.

'Candelaria,' Rosa repeated. 'I was there, you know, that night.'

'I guessed as much.'

'So it's only a matter of time.'

'But why?'

'Because, even though we're all too scared to talk, they can't leave us around. They can't take the chance that someday we'll suddenly find the guts to come forward. So they're just waiting for the right time. You know what happens when we see them, Laura?'

'No.'

'They look at their watches and say, "My, isn't it getting late? Time we did our tidying up and took out the rubbish." Then they laugh and say, "Well, maybe not just yet, but soon."'

'Well, why don't you get out?' asked Laura anxiously. 'Run. Get away.'

'Where? These people have friends everywhere. Do you know about Wagner? He was in hiding, in a "safe house", but they still got to him. Where could I go? Brazil's big, but ....'

'Then leave Brazil. Go to some country where you'd be safe, where they can't get you.'

'Oh, Laura, get real! I don't have any money. Even if I did, I don't have any papers. All I can do is stay here and wait.'

Rosa sounded defeated, fatalistic. 'That's the way it is here. I've heard that one street kid dies every day, in Brazil. A few weeks ago they killed three kids because they couldn't pay the bus fare — the fucking *bus* fare! They just dragged them off the bus and shot them dead. In Rio, being dead is just another way of being. One day it'll be my turn. Big deal.'

There has to be a way, there has to. I can't let her die ....

Suddenly Laura knew what she had to do.

'Can you get papers?' she asked.

'What's the point?'

Laura ignored that. 'I asked, can you get papers? Yes or no?' she said firmly.

'Listen, I told you,' Rosa replied, 'they have friends everywhere. If I tried to get papers, they'd find out. Then they'd come even sooner.'

'Oh, for Christ's sake, stop being so bloody passive,' said Laura angrily. 'There must be some way to get papers. Think!'

'There's Joseph,' said Rosa, sounding shaken by the force of Laura's rebuke. 'He's a forger. If anyone steals a foreigner's handbag, he'll give them twenty reals for the papers. Then he changes them and sells them.'

'Good. Then go to Joseph and get papers,' Laura ordered.

'Oh, sure! What about the money?'

'Forget about the money,' said Laura excitedly. Then she thought again. 'No, find out how much it'll cost. Try to get it as cheap as possible.'

'Why? What's the point?'

'The point is,' said Laura, drawing a deep breath, 'I have a plan to get you out. You have to trust me, but first you have to find out how much your papers will cost.'

For a few seconds there was a stunned silence. When Rosa spoke, Laura could hear hope rising in her voice.

'I'll go right away,' she said. 'I've heard Joseph charges five or six hundred reals for papers, but he's an old man. He likes me.' She giggled. 'He likes watching me walk by in my tight T-shirt and shorts, and he's always asking me to come inside with him for a while. Maybe if I'm very nice to him he'll charge me less.'

Laura understood what she meant. For a moment the thought of an old man rubbing his hands over Rosa's young body made her feel like retching. But she couldn't be judgmental. It was Rosa's choice. She had a right to survive.

'Do what you have to. I don't want to know,' she said. 'Find out the price and get back to me tomorrow.'

'I will, Laura. And thank you. Bye.'

'Bye.'

Laura closed her eyes and rolled over. In the darkness she could just make out the poster for one of her favourite films, *The Power of One*.

She smiled. *The power of one is the power of many.* One person could make a difference. She could make a difference. At least, she hoped she could.

'Sanjid,' she called into the darkness. 'Sanjid, it's Laura.'

'Laura!' came the reply. 'Laura, I'm so glad you called me! When you wouldn't answer I thought you were mad at me. Rosa told me what she did. She was very silly.'

'She was silly,' said Laura softly. 'But it's OK now. I'm better, and we're still friends.'

'I'm glad. I'd hate to lose you.' The little voice sounded tired and frail.

'I'm calling to tell you I have a plan to help Rosa, to get her away.'

'That's good,' said the little voice. 'Thank you.'

He sounds dreadful, thought Laura. *Just like Katie when she had the flu — all weak and listless.*

'Are you OK?' she asked.

'I'm just tired. We're ....' Suddenly the little voice was sobbing. 'Oh please, Laura, please, when you've saved Rosa, please come and save me. I want to go home. I miss my mother and my little sisters and .... The master, Babu Krishna, is really mad — he has a deadline — the agent was here yesterday, yelling that we'd be late with the order. Babu beat us .... We work from dark in the morning until dark at night .... Patit Lal's father came and told Babu to give him back his son, but Babu drove him off with guns .... He beat us again, and ... and ... and ....'

'Sanjid, Sanjid, don't cry,' Laura said, trying to sound calm. 'Please don't cry.'

'Laura, I have to go. He's coming with a big stick. He looks very angry. I have to go.'

'Sanjid ....'

'I have to.'

The voice in her head was gone.

Laura listened to the sound of Katie breathing softly in the dark. Sanjid couldn't be much older than her.

Tears ran down her face, and she bit into the pillow.

'The power of one is the power of change,' she sobbed. 'The power of one is the power of change. I'll make it change for you, Sanjid, Rosa. I don't know how, but I *will*. I promise.'

~

Captain's Log
Monday, 30 October
10.15 p.m.

I have to get them out. I have to. The death squads and Babu Krishna — the bastards .... I have to get them away.

And just a few hours ago I was ready to give up on them because Rosa's glue-sniffing nearly killed me.

I don't care what it takes. I'll get them out.

Some people are such bastards!

chapter
14

Laura drew a big red circle around the figures on the notepad.

£1,475.

It was a king's ransom!

She'd had no idea it would cost that much. Before she'd phoned Aer Lingus, she'd been guessing that a flight from Brazil would cost between five and six hundred pounds, about the same as the return flights to Los Angeles she'd seen advertised in the papers.

But fourteen hundred and seventy-five pounds!

She looked at the figure at the bottom of the page — £350. That was all she had. She'd spent the entire morning drawing up a list of all the money she could raise for Rosa's flight, and that was it: three hundred and fifty pounds. Even if the fare had been only six hundred pounds, she'd still have been two hundred and fifty pounds short.

And now?

She chewed her pencil and reviewed the figures one by one.

She had two hundred and fifty pounds in the bank, money she'd saved over the last two years. If she sold her new bike she'd probably get forty. Her Walkman and all her tapes would probably raise another twenty-five pounds. That brought the figure up to £315. She could sell her jewellery, but she didn't have much, and what she did have wouldn't raise more than five pounds. There was Kev's Nintendo. He didn't use it much, now that he had a computer. She'd probably get twenty pounds for that. (Of course, he'd go crazy when he found out, but she was banking on the fact that he wouldn't find out until Rosa had arrived. Once he'd heard her story, he was sure to be OK — Laura hoped.)

The only other things of any real value that she owned were her cameras and her photography magazines. There were about a hundred magazines. If she could sell them for tenpence each, that would add an extra ten pounds, giving her a grand total of three hundred and fifty pounds. She was eleven hundred and twenty-five pounds short.

She lifted her pen, slowly crossed out '£350', and scribbled in '£700'.

She *could* raise another three hundred and fifty pounds. She'd thought about it during the night, but even thinking about it was painful. She'd rather have sold blood. It would be like selling her babies. But she didn't have a choice. She would have to sell her cameras. Much as she loved them, they weren't people; Rosa was a breathing, flesh-and-blood person, and she was in danger. Laura could always save up to buy other cameras, but this was Rosa's only life.

The Pentax had been a Christmas present from her parents. It was less than a year old, but she'd probably get only about fifty pounds for it. The Bronica would raise a lot more. It had been a gift from her grandfather. He'd bought it out of his retirement money, when Laura had won a prize in the Fuji young photographers' competition. It had been second-hand, but it had still cost six hundred pounds. She'd probably get around three hundred pounds for it.

Seven hundred pounds was still a long way from what she needed, but at least it was a start. She'd find the balance somehow. She'd borrow it, or maybe her parents would help her get a bank loan.

She looked at the ticket price again, and suddenly her heart skipped with delight.

'Why didn't I notice that before?' she said excitedly.

It was just one word, but it made a lot of difference to her calculations. 'Return: £1,475.' Rosa didn't need a return ticket.

'She could stay. Or maybe we can buy the return ticket later. The important thing is to get her out.'

Laura picked up the phone and jabbed excitedly at the numbers. The number was engaged.

'OK, if a one-way ticket is, say, eight hundred and fifty pounds, that leaves us a hundred and fifty pounds short, and .... Oh, damn and double damn! I forgot those bloody papers.' She slammed her fist against the side of the sofa, angry with herself. 'If they cost Rosa three hundred pounds, then that's .... Christ! Eleven hundred and fifty. How could I have forgotten that?'

For a moment she felt deflated.

'No! Stuff it!' she said, with determination. 'I don't care how much it costs. I'll raise it.'

She reached for the phone and dialled again. This time it rang. After six rings it was answered by an answering machine.

'All our operators are busy with other customers at

the moment. We appreciate your call and would ask you to hold for the next available operator. Thank you.'

Laura endured a minute of horrible, electronic 'Home on the Range'; then the operator answered.

'Hello, enquiries and reservations. How may I help you?'

'I ... I was on a few minutes ago, checking out the price of return flights from Rio de Janeiro,' Laura said, feeling rather self-conscious. 'I forgot to ask the price of a one-way flight.'

'And which city in Rio did you want to fly from?'

The question threw Laura. 'It ... it *is* a city, I think,' she replied. 'In Brazil.'

'Of course, sorry,' said the operator without a pause. 'Hold the line and I'll just check.'

Laura winced as 'Home on the Range' began again, but she only had to endure it for a few seconds.

'When would the journey be?'

'This month.'

'And it would be Rio to Dublin?'

'That's right.'

'Well, between now and the end of December a one-way ticket, Rio de Janeiro to Dublin, would be £884, and there would be some duties on top of that — about twenty-five or thirty pounds.'

£914. It was still expensive.

'Would you like to make a provisional booking?' asked the operator helpfully.

'No ... no, thanks. Not at this stage.'

'That's fine. Thank you for your enquiry. Goodbye.'

'Bye.'

She was still two hundred and fourteen pounds short of the fare — and then there was the matter of the passport .... Laura wrote '£214' on her notepad.

Maybe Rosa could be really nice to the old man! she

thought, smiling. Immediately she regretted the thought.

She looked at the figure again. £214. It wasn't *that* much. If she could find ten people who'd each lend her twenty-five pounds, she'd be able to make it, and have a little left over. As for the papers — well, she'd worry about that when she knew the price. For now, she had to find ten people.

She turned the page and began compiling the list. She'd got as far as her parents when the doorbell rang. She went to the door.

'Hi!' said Gnasher. 'Your brother said you were home, and we just thought we'd drop by on our way home for lunch and see how you are.'

'Yeah, we heard it was a bad attack,' added Kelz.

'It was,' said Laura. 'But I'm fine now. Oh, and thanks for the card!'

'That's OK,' they replied together.

'Listen,' said Laura, pushing the door open, 'do you want to come in for a minute?'

'Nah, it's OK,' said Kelz. 'Just thought we'd see how you were. We better get going.'

'OK. See you.'

'See you.'

'Oh, just one thing,' Laura called after them, suddenly realising she had an opportunity.

They turned.

'Listen, I know it's a lot to ask, but I'm looking for ten people to lend me twenty-five pounds each. I can't tell you what it's for — you'll have to trust me — but I will pay you back.'

Gnasher and Kelz looked at each other.

'Sure, why not,' shrugged Gnasher.

'Kelz?'

Kelz thought about it for a second.

'Yeah, why not.' She looked a little embarrassed.

'But will you do us a favour, then?'

'OK.'

'We're putting a band together, and .... Well, would you do some photos of us? I know how good you are.'

'A band! No kidding! Sure,' said Laura. 'I think it's a great idea. I know how good Dave is on piano, and I've heard you sing. I think it'll be great. But there's only one thing ....' She dropped her voice; she had no idea why, but it seemed the right thing to do. 'It'll have to be pretty soon, because I'm selling my cameras.'

'You're what!' said Gnasher in surprise. 'You've gotta be joking. I thought you slept with the bloody things under your pillow.'

Laura laughed, for the first time in almost a week.

'I was never quite that bad, but I have to sell them. I need the money.'

'Well, fair enough,' said Gnasher. 'I suppose you know what you're doing, but I think you're nuts.'

Laura nodded.

'I won't be able to give you the money for a couple of weeks. Is that OK?' said Kelz.

'Sure, no problem.'

'And how much for the photos?' asked Gnasher.

'Well, I've got a couple of spare rolls of black-and-white film. So if you pay for the processing we'll call it quits.'

'That's great,' said Kelz.

'Yeah, but you should think long and hard before you sell your cameras,' cautioned Gnasher.

'I have,' replied Laura. 'Believe me, I have.'

'Fair enough,' he answered. 'Anyway, we'd better get going. See you.'

'See you,' echoed Kelz.

'Yeah, see you,' answered Laura.

As she watched them walk down the avenue, she smiled to herself.

'Two down, eight to go.'

She started to close the door.

'Laura, wait up!'

Conor walked around the hedge, swinging his bag onto his shoulder.

'What did Scumbags Inc. want?' he said, nodding after Gnasher and Kelz.

'More to the point, what does Dickhead Supreme want?' said Laura angrily.

Conor ignored the insult. 'You really shouldn't be messing with that lot.'

'Look, Conor, if you've got a point, get to it. Otherwise, just piss off and take your ego somewhere else.'

'My, aren't we narky?' he laughed. 'I was —'

'Hi, Laura! Just called in to see how you were .... Oh, hi, Conor!'

As Sarah came up the path, Laura noticed that she'd removed her school tie and unbuttoned three buttons of her blouse to show the top of her cleavage.

'I heard you were sick, and I thought I'd drop in to see how you were.'

'Yeah, sure you did,' said Laura under her breath.

Sarah flicked her hair and let her hand move slowly down her neck to the button on her blouse.

What a prat, thought Laura. Then she thought of her 'hit list' and smiled. Sarah wasn't on it, because under normal circumstances getting her to spend money on something other than herself would be like getting blood out of a stone; but with Conor there to be impressed ....

'Sarah, I have to raise money for something, a very worthy cause, and I was just wondering — would you donate twenty-five pounds, in return for that photo session I did for you the other Saturday?'

'Twenty-five pounds! I haven't got that sort of money ....' Sarah began.

'But you spent more than that on your bra-and-pants set,' said Laura.

'But that was different. And anyway, your photo sessions are always for nothing, and —'

'Of course you've got money,' Conor snapped at Sarah. 'You're loaded. You've always got cash.'

'Yeah, but it's normally ....'

Laura smiled. She was beginning to enjoy herself.

Sarah glared at her. 'Well, I suppose I could,' she said, trying to smile sweetly. 'But it'll take me a couple of days to —'

'There,' said Laura, trying not to look too triumphant. 'That wasn't too hard, was it? Conor will lend it to me and you can pay him back — isn't that right, Conor?'

'I .... Yeah, sure,' Conor stammered. 'Listen, Laura, I need to talk to you about something. Can I come in?'

'Well, I'm still feeling very weak,' Laura lied. 'We can have a chat here at the door, but it'll have to be quick.'

Conor turned to Sarah and smiled. 'Listen, Sash, this is really personal. Would you mind leaving us alone?'

Sarah flushed.

'No — no, that's OK,' she said, trying to hide her embarrassment. 'I have to go anyway. See you later, Conor.'

She didn't even look at Laura.

For a second, Laura felt a sting of sympathy as she watched Sarah go; but then she remembered the conversation she'd overheard in the toilets, and the sympathy dissolved.

'How much money do you need?' asked Conor seriously.

'Oh, just a couple of hundred quid,' said Laura.

'For what?'

'I can't say.'

'Well, OK — that's your business. But I'll tell you what I'll do.'

Conor dropped his voice and glanced around. 'I'm putting this really sweet deal together, and I'll cut you in, as a friend.'

Laura wanted to laugh. *This really sweet deal? The prat thinks he's some whizzkid wheeler-dealer!*

'I can guarantee to double any money you kick in, in less than a week. If I don't, I'll give you back every penny. Interested?'

'Interested!' said Laura, delighted. It was the answer to all her problems. If Conor could double her money, she'd have enough to get Rosa out before the end of the week.

'Sure, I'm interested,' she said, 'but how can you do that?'

'It's easy,' said Conor. 'I've got this pal at university, and he can get me any amount of hash I want, at a real low price. I sell it off to the scumbags here, and ....'

It took Laura a second to realise what he was proposing, and another microsecond to consider and reject the idea. Then she exploded.

'Are you insane?' she snapped at him. 'You're standing here, on my doorstep, asking me to become' — she dropped her voice and hissed at him — 'a drug dealer. You must be out of your tiny mind!'

'But, Laura, it's only hash —'

'Conor, fuck off!' she said sharply. 'Just fuck off and never come near me again.'

She slammed the door, leaving him standing on the doorstep.

'Laura, Laura,' called Conor, tapping softly on the door. 'I was only joking. Honest. Open the door and let me explain.'

Laura went into the kitchen and shut the door.

What a nerve! What a dickhead!

Then she started laughing.

She'd done it! She'd lost her temper at someone without feeling the slightest hint of regret. The only regret she had was that, for a second, she'd actually considered his suggestion.

chapter
15

Laura poked her head around the kitchen door. Half of the table was covered by the history essays Joe was correcting. He was smiling at some of the answers he was reading. Chris was copying notes from a book and looking very serious. Laura looked at the title. *Death and the Child: A Coping Strategy.* (*Jesus! No wonder she looks so serious. That's hardly a bundle of laughs.*)

'Hey, Lar,' said her dad, looking up. 'Did you know that Ferdinand Magellan was the first man to circumcise the globe? Or that Christopher Columbus discovered Americans?'

'And Joan of Arc was Noah's wife,' laughed Laura, quoting one of her favourite films.

'How are you feeling?' asked Chris. 'You're looking a bit better.'

'Fine, I'm fine,' said Laura.

She'd been trying to think of a way to ask them all day. She didn't want to lie to them, but she didn't want to tell them the truth either; she knew it would just lead to questions she couldn't answer, not yet.

'Listen, I've got a favour to ask you,' she said, trying not to make eye contact with either of them.

'Go ahead. As Mr Spock would say, I'm all ears,' answered her father.

Laura and her mother groaned at the joke, which they'd heard about a million times.

'The thing is, I'm trying to raise money for a Third World thing. I can't tell you what it is just yet.' Laura paused, waiting to see if they would ask any questions. They didn't, so she carried on. 'It's quite a lot of money, actually — about fifteen hundred pounds.'

Joe gave a little cough and shrugged his shoulders. 'Oh, is that all? No problem! We'll sell Kev.'

'Joe,' said Chris, softly but firmly. 'She's being serious.' She turned to Laura. 'That's a lot of money, Lar. And you don't want to tell us exactly what you're raising it for?'

'Not just yet,' Laura said. 'But it's a good cause, and I think you'll be pleased. You just have to trust me.'

'You know we do,' said her father. 'But we couldn't raise that sort of money at the moment.'

'That's the good thing,' replied Laura. 'You don't have to. I've made a list of all the things I can sell and how much I expect to get for them.'

She handed the list to her mother. Chris glanced at it quickly and looked up in surprise.

'Your cameras, Lar? You can't be serious.'

'I am, Mom, dead serious. This is much too important. I can always find the money for new cameras, but this has to be done soon!' Laura heard the urgency creeping into her voice.

'It really is that important to you, and that urgent?' asked her father.

'It is, honest.'

Her parents looked at each other quickly.

'Listen, Lar, they're your cameras. If this is that important to you, do what you need to do,' said Chris.

'And what do we have to do?' asked Joe. 'We haven't got that much money at the moment.'

'Look.' Laura gave him her hit list. 'I've made a list of ten people. If they each kick in twenty-five pounds, I should have more or less what I need for the first part of what I'm going to do.'

Joe looked at the list quietly and then passed it to his wife.

'You know, Lar,' he said, 'your figures only add up to about eight hundred, even if everybody kicks in, which isn't certain. That's still a fair bit short.'

'I know,' said Laura anxiously. 'But I was hoping that if there's any shortfall, you would be my guarantor for a bank loan.'

'And you still don't want to tell us what it's for?' asked her father softly.

'I can't, Dad, honest!'

'Does it have anything to do with all this stuff you've been reading about street kids?'

Laura nodded.

'Well, then ....' He looked at Chris. She nodded without hesitation.

'OK, we'll kick in the shortfall, provided it's not more than a couple of hundred pounds. You can either pay it all back, or pay part of it back and work off the balance by doing extra odd jobs — cleaning the car, doing the garden, painting some of the woodwork.'

'That's bonded labour, but thanks a million,' said Laura, laughing. She ran over and gave them each a huge hug. 'You won't regret this, I promise.'

'We know,' said her mother.

'Hey, maybe you can come in and teach my nippers,' suggested her father. 'They don't seem to be learning much history from me.'

'Why not,' smiled Laura, on her way to the door. 'Caesar is a salad and Napoleon is a short dead dude.'

'Thank you, Bill and Ted,' replied her father, turning back to his marking.

~

Laura was feeling elated. It was all coming together.

So far, everyone she'd contacted from her hit list had agreed to give her the twenty-five pounds, albeit unwillingly in Sarah's case. Conor had actually given her thirty, pushing the money into her hand with a mumbled 'Sorry about earlier,' as he arrived at the house for history tuition from her father. But the real surprise had been Gnasher's phone call in the afternoon.

'Hey, Laura, Gnasher here. Guess what?'

'What?'

'I've got you another thirty-five pounds.'

'You what!'

'And I bet you didn't know you had a secret admirer, did you?'

'I've got hundreds,' Laura laughed.

'Well, this one must be really keen. He heard me and Kelz talking about you selling your cameras to raise money, when we were in the library ....'

'Dave!'

'What's the surprise for — because we were in the library, or because we were indiscreet enough to get overheard?'

'Both,' said Laura. 'I don't want everyone to know.'

'Yeah, I know, and I'm sorry. We didn't see him, though Christ knows how we missed a big fucker like him. Anyway, he said he hadn't meant to eavesdrop, but he couldn't help hearing, and he wondered why you were selling them.'

'So you told him?'

'Well, I couldn't tell him much, could I? I don't *know* exactly why you're doing it. I just said you were doing it to raise money for something, some cause or other, I guessed.'

It was only when Laura heard it like that that she realised just how trusting Gnasher and Kelz were being. They hadn't a clue why she needed the money, but they were each still prepared to give her twenty-five pounds.

'Anyway, I told him we were donating thirty-five quid each.'

'Thirty-five! But —'

'Yeah, I know. But there was method in the madness. Anyway, he said he'd kick in thirty-five pounds too, and he'll give it to me by the end of the week.'

'You're a real scam artist!'

'Thanks. That's the nicest thing anyone's said to me in days.'

'But why you? Why won't he give it to me?'

'I don't know. Maybe he thinks you'd be embarrassed, or he'd be embarrassed. This guy's weird anyway.'

'Weird?'

'Well, nice weird, but for his own reasons he doesn't want you to know. Shame, really, because from the little I know of him I think he'd suit you a lot better than that prat you hang around with.'

'I don't hang around with Conor. He's just my badminton partner.'

'Well, someone should tell him that. He acts like you're an item.'

'Believe me, he knows very well that we're no item.'

Suddenly Laura had an idea. It was something she

hadn't thought about till that moment, but it was an essential part of her plan, and for some reason Gnasher seemed to be the right person to ask.

'Listen, scam-master, I want to ask you something, but I want you to swear not to mention it to anyone.'

'Why all the secrecy?'

It was a good question, and Laura wasn't really sure of the answer. After all, she was sure that, if she announced that she was trying to save the life of a street kid in Brazil, she'd receive great support. But she couldn't. Maybe it was because she'd shared Rosa's fear at the thought of what would happen if the wrong people found out; or maybe she just didn't want anyone to know because ... because .... She wasn't sure. It just seemed better to keep it between her and Rosa.

'I can't really tell you, but I just think it's important.'

'This is real James Bond stuff, but OK. I swear. I won't tell a soul, 007.'

'Not even Barbara?'

There was silence on the other end of the phone.

'Dave?'

'Well, I don't know about that. She can read me like a book. I don't know if I could keep a secret from her.'

Laura thought for a second.

'OK, but promise you'll try — and if you can't, then get her to promise not to tell.'

'OK.'

'Now, this is a simple question. How could I get money or an airline ticket to someone in Brazil, without the authorities finding out?'

'Is that what this is all about?' Gnasher asked. 'Candelaria?'

'How do you know —' Laura began, amazed.

'I was there, remember? In Amnesty. I was the one who had to sort out the requests, and there was only one request the evening you were there. Of course, it didn't have to be you, but ....' He let the words trail off.

'Yeah. That's exactly what this is about. But don't —'

'It's OK. I won't say a word. Not even to Barbara. Promise.'

He paused for a second. 'Laura?'

'What?'

'You're incredible, do you know that? You and your secret admirer have more in common than you could ever imagine. I'll get back to you in ten minutes.'

The phone went dead before she could reply.

Laura liked the idea of a secret admirer, even if Gnasher's descriptions of him as 'a big fucker' and 'weird' weren't exactly flattering. Who could it be? Gnasher hadn't given her much to work on. She could think of a few people in school who fitted one description or the other, but none who fitted both. Maybe the clue was in Gnasher's comment, 'You have more in common than you could ever imagine.' Maybe that meant he was in Third World First or Greenpeace or one of the other school societies Laura was in, but no one came to mind.

Jesus, she laughed to herself. *You're so conceited, Laura Byrne! Two people you know about are having a really rough time, and all you can do is try to figure out who might fancy you. Cop on!*

She'd hardly finished the thought before Gnasher was back on the phone.

'Laura, how well do you know the Franciscans in town?'

'Not at all. Why?'

'Well, I just rang a friend at Amnesty and told him I was writing a story in which someone has to get money to someone in Brazil secretly, but I couldn't figure out how to do it, and —'

'And?' Laura asked eagerly.

'And he reckons if it was him, he'd try the Franciscans, or one of the other missionary orders, because they have missions and workers all over Brazil. So you give them the money here, they phone their place in Rio and ask them to give the same amount to whoever comes to collect it, and that's it. A bit like a courier service, really.'

'You're bloody brilliant, Dave, do you know that?' Laura exploded with delight.

'Yeah, I'm afraid you're right,' Gnasher laughed.

'Honest!'

'I'm being honest.'

'Listen, thanks a million. That's really great.'

'Pleased to have been of service. Anything else you need done — washing-up, laundry, cheese soufflé — just give me a call. Bye.'

'Bye.'

Laura went upstairs and lay on her bed. It was all coming together, it really was. The money was in place — well, almost — and, thanks to Gnasher, she had a way to get it to Rosa without anyone finding out. She had to tell her.

chapter
16

Laura closed her eyes and concentrated on the spot in the centre of her forehead.

'Rosa,' she called silently. 'Rosa, it's Laura. Can you hear me?'

'Yeah, I hear you.'

'Have you seen Joseph about your papers yet?' asked Laura, trying to control her excitement.

'Yeah, I saw him,' replied Rosa. 'If I'm nice to him, he'll get me papers for two hundred reals.' She giggled. 'Maybe if I'm *very* nice, he'll let me have them for less.'

Laura ignored the implication. 'When can he have them ready?'

'He took some photos today, lots.' Again she giggled, giving the sentence a different meaning. 'And he said if I had the money, the papers could be ready in three days.'

'Three days!' Laura couldn't contain her excitement any longer. 'Three days,' she repeated, laughing. 'Then

you could be here by next week, if I get everything
ready.'

'Laura, you do really mean it, don't you?' asked
Rosa breathlessly. 'It isn't a joke?'

'No. It isn't a joke. I can have all the money by tomorrow, and then .... I'll find a way to have everything
ready for you.'

'You mustn't send anything to me, Laura,' Rosa
cautioned. 'They'll find out, or it could be stolen, or —'

'I've thought of that. It'll be fine. I promise.'

She could hear Rosa beginning to cry. Then a voice
was calling to her, softly.

'That's Nanna,' said Rosa. 'She thinks I'm upset, but
Laura, I'm overwhelmed. This is so incredible — if I
don't go out and walk I'll burst with laughter.' She
stopped. 'D'you want to see what I'll be leaving?'

Laura didn't reply. Rosa understood the silence.

'I swear on the Virgin I won't do anything stupid
this time.'

'If you really swear.'

'I swear, nothing will happen.'

'OK.'

'Then close your eyes really tight.'

Laura closed her eyes tightly. This time there wasn't
any pain as the blue light poured in.

Slowly, a face came into focus.

The face was dark and wrinkled; it reminded Laura
of the old leather armchair in the den. But even in the
dim light she could see that the most prominent feature
of the face was the eyes — eyes so brown that they
were almost black, eyes that danced with life. As she
grew accustomed to the dark, Laura could see that the
face was framed by long silver hair that flowed over
the shoulders and down to the waist.

'Nanna,' said Rosa, identifying the old lady, who

rocked back and forth cuddling a baby in her arms.

Nanna kept up an almost continuous flow of speech directed towards Rosa, punctuating it every now and then with a laugh that rocked her body and showed her almost toothless mouth.

'She's not really my Nanna,' Rosa explained. 'She took my mom off the streets when she was just a kid. But my mom got involved with drug dealers and left home a while back. She's dead now. They found her body in a dumpster. But I'll stay with Nanna for ever.'

Rosa stopped, suddenly realising that she too would soon be leaving Nanna. Laura could feel her sadness.

'It'll only be for a little while,' she said comfortingly. 'Just till it's safe.'

'Yeah,' sighed Rosa. 'Just till it's safe.'

Rosa stretched a hand towards the old rusting fridge beside her; as she opened it, the door came off in her hand. Nanna said something, laughing.

'She says I shouldn't damage the antiques — I'll lower their worth at auction,' Rosa giggled. Laura laughed too.

Rosa took a piece of bread from the almost-empty fridge, then lifted the door and replaced it carefully.

She turned, as slowly as a camera panning the room, so that Laura could see everything. The room was tiny, probably no bigger than the Byrnes' 'study'. Two sets of bunks stood against one wall. On one of the top bunks, a boy about Kev's age was flicking through a comic. Below him a little boy and girl were playing tug-of-war with a rag doll. A child of about four was sitting on the other bottom bunk, swinging his legs aimlessly.

Nanna sat on an old rocking-chair, comforting the baby. Behind her, two teenage boys lounged on an old sofa, watching cartoons on an old black-and-white television. Another old sofa was sandwiched between the open door and a small two-ring stove; Laura guessed that that was where Rosa had been sitting. Two girls about Katie's age were curled up on the sofa, asleep.

'There are sixteen of us here,' said Rosa proudly. 'None of us are Nanna's, but she looks after us all. Her own kids are bigger; they live in a different part of the favela.'

'Favela?'

'Our district, our — our shantytown, I guess you'd call it. They live in another part of our shantytown. Sometimes Nanna's grandchildren come to visit.'

There was a quick interchange between Rosa and Nanna. Rosa hugged her, then turned quickly and said something to the boys on the sofa. The boys laughed and threw a cushion at her, chanting 'Freddy, Freddy, Freddy.'

Rosa caught the cushion, threw it back at them and jumped quickly through the doorway.

They were walking along a narrow lane. On their left was a row of makeshift little wooden dwellings like the one Rosa lived in. To their right was a high brick wall.

The whole area seemed to be alive with people of all ages. Their colours spanned the whole spectrum, from very black to fair-skinned. A group of women were washing their clothes in a row of sinks that ran along the wall. Every now and then a boy would run past, shouting something that made the women jump up screaming.

'The boys are messing with the women,' said Rosa. 'They keep telling them there are rats in the drain.'

'Rats!' Laura could feel the hairs on the back of her neck standing up.

'Yeah, sure, the little bastards are all over the place,'

said Rosa. 'But we mostly see them when it's dark. They swim down there, in the drain.'

She peered towards a small open drain that ran the full length of the wall. It was clogged with domestic waste and excrement, and the water from the sinks skimmed along the top, flooding out into the alleyway. Laura felt her stomach churning.

Rosa carried on.

'At night the rats run over the feet of the women washing. You can hear them running over the roofs of the houses. Sometimes they come into the houses and bite people's ears. That's never happened in our house. I heard about this woman who had a kid that was deaf and dumb, so it couldn't cry, and the rats ate its nose. That might be just bullshit, though, like the story about Crazy Mary's kid.'

Even though her stomach was churning, Laura had to hear more.

'Who's Crazy Mary?'

They had left the crowded alleyway and were heading down a long flight of steps that ran along the side of the favela. The steps seemed to go on for ever.

'We might see her tonight, when we head into the square,' said Rosa. 'She lives in the sewers.'

'She lives underground?' said Laura incredulously.

'Yeah, sure,' said Rosa, sounding surprised that Laura was surprised. 'Lots of people do. It's warm, it's safe, and nobody gives you hassle.'

'But aren't there rats?'

'Thousands of them. Some people say the sewer kids treat them like pets and train them to be like guard dogs, but I think that's bullshit. I've been down there plenty of times, and I've never seen one of those fuckers that looked friendly. Anyway, if what Crazy Mary says is true, they're anything but friendly.'

Rosa paused, waiting for Laura to reply. When no reply came she carried on.

'Crazy Mary says the rats stole her baby while she was asleep. But I don't believe that either. I reckon Marco sold it to baby-buyers.'

Laura was too stunned to reply.

'If he did, the kid's probably in America now, having a great life.'

At the bottom of the steps, Rosa headed towards an open field. In a distant corner of the field was a small, dark hill; Laura could see figures moving around on it. As they came closer, she saw that the hill was made of rubbish and that the figures — mostly children, but some older men — were hunting through the rubbish and piling things into plastic bags.

Rosa sensed her unasked question.

'They're looking for stuff to sell,' she offered. 'Cans or bottles they can sell to dealers, clothes, bits of furniture, that kind of stuff. Once my brother Raphael — he's not my real brother, he just lives with Nanna — he found a fucking *gold watch*. I swear to God. It must've come from one of the hotels. It was still working and everything. He sold it for fifteen reals.'

The children were scampering around in the rubbish as if it was an adventure playground. Here and there a scrawny dog was rooting for food. Laura watched a dog with a live rat in its mouth running in circles around a group of little boys, who were playing football with the skull of some animal.

'We're crossing here.'

A small plank lay across the open sewer that separated the edge of the rubbish tip from a piece of waste ground that sloped down to the road. As Rosa carefully crossed the plank, she looked down; the carcass of a dead dog was floating in the stagnant sewage below them. A little way beyond the edge of the plank, a collection of old boxes and crates were grouped together. Laura could see smoke rising from behind them.

As Rosa skipped down from the plank, Laura was startled to see an old man sitting among the boxes, frying bread in a pan over an open fire. Faces peered out from inside the boxes. 'Yeah, they live there,' said Rosa, answering Laura's unasked question.

As they walked, Rosa kept up a constant stream of chat. It reminded Laura of the guided tours of Old Kilkenny or Viking Dublin that she'd been on with the school. For every place she went, Rosa seemed to have some story.

'Those apartments are where the rich bastards live. Sometimes we can hear the noise of their parties in the favela. If you're standing in the right place, you can see them on their balconies drinking champagne or whatever they drink ....'

'The Mardi Gras parade comes along here at the start of Lent ....'

'Up that way is Aterro do Flamengo Gardens, where they shot Wagner and the others ....'

'That's the old Buddhist's house. He's nice to us. Sometimes he lets us come in and talk and gives us food ....'

Everywhere they went, there seemed to be children — roaming around, sleeping in doorways, sitting on the edge of the road doing nothing in particular — and Rosa seemed to know everyone.

'That guy with the nice body is Philip. He's a shoeshine boy. I used to fancy him, but he's turned into a real asshole; he has this racket where he gets other kids, little kids, to hire shoeshine gear off him, and then he takes most of what they earn .... That guy leaning against the wall, that's Max — the best pickpocket in

Rio, but a real stingy bastard. He wouldn't give you a real if you were starving .... That's Gina. Sometimes she cleans car windows, other times she keeps the men tourists happy — you know what I mean, right?'

Laura knew what she meant.

'She's fifteen and she's already got two kids. They're gorgeous, but ....' Rosa let the sentence trail off.

In between pointing out places and people, she punctuated her chat with excited questions about Ireland.

'And when I get there, will I live with you?'

Laura hadn't thought about that, but she presumed so. 'Yes, you can share a room with me and Katie.'

'The two of you have a room to yourselves?'

'Yeah. Kev has his own.'

'Who's Kev?'

'My brother. He's fifteen.'

'And is he cute?'

'I don't know! Yeah, I suppose so — in a way.'

'Maybe I can share his room, then!' Rosa giggled. 'If it's cold, I'll need someone to keep me warm at night.'

'Rosa!'

'What? I could teach him things.'

'Yeah, and I can guess what you have in mind!' Laura giggled.

'Are Irish boys good-looking? Are they passionate?'

'Jesus, Rosa, don't you ever think about anything else?'

'No. Well, sometimes. But are they? Are they sexy?'

'Well, I know at least one who thinks he is.'

'Your boyfriend?'

'God, no. I wouldn't go out with Conor if I was paid.'

'Well, maybe I can.'

'You're welcome to him — if you can prise Sarah off of him.'

'No problem to me!'

'No, I reckon it wouldn't be,' said Laura, grinning.

God! Having her here sounds like it'll be some experience.

'I'm so excited about it all, Laura. I can't wait to be there.'

The only time Rosa's chatter stopped was when they walked into a cobbled area in front of a church. Laura could feel her mood change as she looked around the large open area. Someone had drawn the outlines of bodies lying on the ground, in red paint.

Laura didn't have to ask. She knew where she was: Candelaria.

She could feel Rosa's memories. The sound of the cars screeching into the square. Doors opening. Masked men, their boots rattling against the cobblestones as they ran. The children looking up — at first in interest, then with panic rising in their breasts as they saw the men raising their automatic weapons to their waists. The terrifying realisation of what was about to happen. Chaos, children running and screaming. Then the sound of gunfire echoing across the square. She heard the screams of those who had been shot and the groans of the dying. She saw the little rivulets of blood flowing among the hard, worn stones of the square.

'Rosa,' she called softly. 'Let's go away from here. We can't bring them back.'

Rosa sighed sadly. 'I know, but we can't forget them either.'

Then she laughed. 'Laura, let me show you something.'

She raced across the square to a manhole cover in the far corner. She lifted it effortlessly.

'Look. This is where some of them kept clothes, or anything they didn't want stolen — it's our safety-deposit box!'

Laura could see the jumpers and jackets thrown in carelessly. To one side, carefully wrapped in plastic,

was a little green teddy bear. It seemed terribly poign-
ant, sitting there on its own.

'Do they have covers like this in Ireland?' asked Rosa.

'I'm sure they do,' replied Laura. 'I never really
noticed.'

They crossed the square and headed down a street
leading off it.

'Tell me about Ireland, about your home and your
family.'

'Where do I start?'

'Anywhere. Tell me about Kev.'

'He's a pain in the neck most times, but sometimes
he can be really sweet ....'

Laura didn't know where they were going; they
could have been walking around in circles, for all she
knew. She talked for about fifteen minutes. She'd never
known she had so much to say.

Occasionally, Rosa would stop her and ask something. It seemed to Laura that the question she repeated
most often was, 'And will I have my own bed, in a
room with just you and Katie?' Laura smiled every
time she heard it. She took something like that for
granted; but for Rosa, who shared a one-room shack
with fifteen other people, it must have seemed like a
real luxury.

They reached the waste ground beyond the rubbish
tip. In the distance, the old man was still sitting by the
fire. Beyond him, children played around the top of the
tip as people sifted the rubbish.

Laura could feel Rosa's excitement. She was almost
shaking, like Katie on Christmas Eve.

'Laura, I'm too excited to sleep, but I'm going home
anyway. I'll get a final price from Joseph tomorrow, and
then I'll contact you and .... I swear, Laura, I'm so
delighted I think I'm going to wet myself!'

There was the sharp sound of a car skidding to a halt, and Laura heard a rough, laughing voice calling something.

She felt the sudden rush of Rosa's fear.

'Laura, a friend's just come. We have to break,' lied Rosa, trying to hide her feelings under a calm voice.

'No, we have to —'

Laura felt a sharp pain in her forehead and snapped her eyes open. She was in her own room, with the light shining softly on her posters. Katie rolled over, making the bedsprings creak. Somewhere in the distance Laura heard a word. One word, vague, almost woolly. 'Freddy.'

It sent a shiver of fear down her spine.

~

Captain's Log
Tuesday, 31 October
10.45 p.m.

I've seen Candelaria and I've felt Rosa's memories of that night. But soon she'll be here, and hopefully we can help her heal. She won't forget the people who died — she doesn't want to — but maybe we can make the pain a little easier.

Why do I feel nervous? Maybe it's just excitement. I don't know. I should be happy but I feel uneasy. It'll be better tomorrow, when I talk to the Franciscans about sending the money.

chapter 17

Laura looked at the luminous hands on the *Toy Story* clock hanging above Katie's bed. It was 4.15 in the morning. She'd been calling to Rosa since midnight. She'd checked in the telephone directory earlier: Brazil was four hours behind Ireland. So it was midnight there.

She called again. 'Rosa? Rosa, it's Laura. Don't block me out.'

The reply didn't come. Laura knew she was being blocked, and it made her anxious.

Freddy .... She'd heard the kids chanting the name as Rosa left her home, and she was convinced she'd heard Rosa mutter the name as the link was broken. Who the hell was he? Why wouldn't Rosa respond?

Laura remembered the promise: 'I swear on the Virgin I won't do anything stupid this time.' Maybe that was why she wouldn't respond. Maybe she was doing something stupid.

Laura wanted to believe it, but she couldn't. She'd felt the fear that Rosa had tried to hide.

Dublin was four hours ahead of Brazil but five hours behind India. Maybe Sanjid had spoken to Rosa. Laura closed her eyes and called softly into the dark.

'Sanjid. Sanjid, it's Laura. Can you hear me?'

'Laura! Where were you? Why wouldn't you or Rosa answer me?' said the little voice in her head, sharply. 'I was calling you both for ages when I finished working. Why didn't you answer? I was scared. I needed you.'

He sounded more angry than anxious. Once, when she was younger, Katie had got lost in the supermarket, and when they'd found her she'd greeted them with a furious 'Where were you?' before bursting into tears. That was how Sanjid sounded.

Laura felt guilty, but it wasn't her fault. She hadn't known that the sharp pain in her head had been Sanjid, any more than Rosa had. If they had, they would have broken the link and one of them would have talked to him.

'So you haven't talked to Rosa?' Laura asked.

'I told you, I tried to find you both but you wouldn't answer. I thought you'd just stopped talking to me, like Patrice did.'

'I'm sorry. We were talking about my plans to get Rosa away.'

There was no reply.

'Sanjid?'

'I'm sorry I was angry,' said the little voice. 'But I got scared and I wanted to talk. Patit's father came back. We could hear them arguing outside. He said he wanted his son back or he'd go to the authorities. But Babu just called him a filthy untouchable and threw money at him and told him it was an advance, and he could only have Patit back when he'd paid off the loan. Then the men with guns chased him away again. When Babu Krishna came back, he was so mad that he beat Patit and threw him into the hole — that's this little space under the floor where he hides us when the authorities come. He says if there's any more trouble like that, he'll kill us all. Laura, please come and take me away. I'm scared.'

Laura could feel his fear, but she didn't know what she could say that would comfort him.

'Sanjid, why don't you and Patit just leave? He can't keep you there if you don't want to stay.'

'Don't be silly,' Sanjid replied sharply. 'You know he can. He can keep us here as long as he wants. He bought us, so he owns us.'

'Bought!' Laura almost screamed the word. 'Bought you!' *This is even worse than bonded labour. This is slavery!*

'Well, not me or the other kids from my village, but Patit and some of the others were bought from the barber.'

Laura couldn't understand what she was hearing; she could only repeat the words. 'Bought from the barber?'

'Didn't I tell you about Patit?' asked Sanjid sadly. 'One day, when their parents were all at work in the stone quarries, the barber in their village said he'd take some of the kids to a cinema. He gave them biscuits and put them in the back of his van and promised he'd bring them home before their parents got back from the quarries. But he didn't take them to a cinema. He drove them all day and all night and brought them here and sold them to Babu. That was ages ago. Now Patit's dad wants him back. That makes Babu really angry and he beats us. But Patit's dad won't give up. He kept yelling that his son's worth more than any barber's new motorcycle, and that he'll be back.'

'Motorcycle!' Laura gasped. 'That bastard sold them so he could buy a motorcycle?'

'It sounds like it,' replied Sanjid. 'I've heard of other kids who were sold for things like that.'

'And — and were you ....' Laura was too close to tears to finish the sentence.

'No, I wasn't sold. My family's really poor. One day this agent came to my village and he got my dad drunk. He told him that if he sent me to make carpets, I'd make loads of money and it would all be sent home to help my family. Then he gave my father five hundred rupees and ....'

Sanjid began to sob.

'Oh, Laura, when you've rescued Rosa, come for me. I want to go home. I miss my mother ....'

'I will, I will,' Laura cried, meaning it. 'I promise I will, but, Sanjid —'

Sanjid's frightened voice cut her sentence short. 'Laura, I have to go. He's angry, and —'

'Sanjid —'

'Laura, I've got to go.'

'Sanjid, don't send me away. Let me stay with you for a while,' said Laura urgently.

'But if I make a mistake he'll beat me, and —'

'You don't have to say anything. Just let me join with you, like I did with Rosa. You'll hardly know I'm there.'

'All right,' said the tired little voice. 'Rosa told me how to do this. Shut your eyes tight.'

Laura closed her eyes. She felt that intense pain in her forehead; she squeezed her eyes tight and rubbed her forehead to ease the pain. A brilliant blue light poured into the spot; then, slowly, the light began to fade, but all Laura could see was dim images.

'I can't see,' she whispered.

'Shhh. You'll get used to it.'

Slowly Laura began to understand the shadowy images. In front of her she could see the strings of a loom. Small brown hands moved nimbly across the frame, pulling coloured wools around the strings, knotting them, then cutting them close to the strings and patting them down with a broad, sharp, rounded knife. The hands worked so quickly that in the few seconds it took for Laura's eyes to adjust, the hands had created a small row of eight knots.

Through the strings, Laura could see other frames. Two or three boys sat at each frame, knotting wool around the strings. They all looked as if they were between Katie's age and Kev's.

The boy immediately in front of Laura was so thin that his shoulder-blades and backbone stood out through his skin. He looked like photos she had seen of people in concentration camps.

'That's Patit,' said Sanjid.

Suddenly, the fragile shoulders hunched and the boy went into a spasm of coughing. He sounded like one of the old men on the bus to town, almost retching to clear their lungs.

'He's choking,' Laura said, panicking. 'Help him!'

Sanjid didn't move.

'Help him,' she called again, urgently.

She could hear shouting and the sound of running feet. Two large, dark hands grabbed the boy around the neck, yanking him violently out of his place.

'Babu Krishna,' said Sanjid.

He looked up, and Laura watched in horror as the big man dragged the boy across the shed, kicked the door open and threw him roughly onto the ground. Then she saw the cane in his hand beating down mercilessly against the naked chest. The boy screamed, and even though she couldn't understand the language, Laura knew he was begging for mercy, between coughs.

'Oh, Sanjid,' Laura cried, almost sobbing. 'You have to run, get away.'

'How?'

Sanjid lifted his head. Babu Krishna was still at the door.

'Look, Laura,' he said.

He looked slowly around the room. Laura could see a single bulb hanging down from the ceiling. The only other light was from one window, set high in the wall. The window was barred. There were six other looms in the room. The only entrance or exit was the door. Laura could see padlocks and chains hanging from the door-frame.

'They lock you in!'

Sanjid heard her surprise.

'We're locked in every night. We sleep down there.' He looked down, lifted his legs and rolled onto his side. Laura was looking into a small trench that ran the full width of the loom. The finished carpet was falling into the trench, and the pieces of cut wool were scattered all along the bottom.

'Sometimes we have rags to cover us. Sometimes we don't.'

'But what if you're sick? Isn't there somewhere — a bed, or ....'

'If we get sick, we stay sick till we get better or die, like Nageshwar did when he got sick.'

Laura couldn't believe how matter-of-fact he was about it. She wanted to urge him to fight, to escape, but how could he?

'Please, Laura, help me get away. I don't want to die here like Nageshwar did.'

'I will, I promise ....'

Sanjid straightened up. The master was dragging
Patit Lal back into the shed. The boy was weeping, and
his side and stomach were covered in large ugly marks
where he had been lashed. His hands were bleeding.

Babu took a match from his pocket and scraped
some of the head into the boy's cuts. Then he lit another match and held it against the match-powder in
the boy's flesh. Laura heard the quick 'phut' as the
powder ignited. Then she heard the boy scream.

'That's to burn the wound closed, so blood won't
get on the carpets,' said Sanjid. Then he was almost
sobbing. 'Please, Laura. Patit looks like he mightn't last
till his father can get him out .... Please come for me ....'

'I will. I promise.'

'Go now,' said Sanjid urgently. 'He's looking at me,
and he looks angry. Go.'

The contact was broken.

'Oh, Jesus, sweet Jesus, if you hear me,' Laura sobbed,
'I'll do anything if you let me get him away from there.
Jesus, Buddha, Saint Francis ... anybody, help him!'

She took out her diary and wrote down everything
she had seen. As she wrote, her tears stained the pages.
She fell asleep with her diary clutched to her chest.

chapter
18

Laura didn't have to go to school — her parents had left the decision up to her — but she went anyway. She knew that if she stayed at home she'd spend the day worrying about Sanjid and Rosa. At least school would provide her with a distraction for half the day. But it was a struggle to stay awake.

She'd tried contacting Rosa again, but she wasn't getting through. She'd been tempted to call Sanjid, in case he had heard from Rosa, but she'd seen the brutality of his master. She couldn't afford to distract him; if she caused him to make a mistake, he could end up being beaten senseless, just like Patit Lal.

The world's so fucking unfair. Street kids, death squads, little slave boys with brutal masters — and all the other crap in the papers: child soldiers, child prostitutes, child .... The list's endless. Why doesn't someone do something?

Laura shook her head, trying to keep herself awake. Conor was on his feet, rambling inanely as he tried to bluff his way through an oral book report on *Ecstasy*, a book of short stories by Ré Ó Laighléis.

'I think the dilemma facing the central character in the story ....'

'Which one?' asked Mr Brady.

'The ... the older one.'

'Which *story*, Mr Meade?'

'The one about ... about the guy who, you know ....'

'Actually, I probably do know, Mr Meade,' said Mr Brady sharply. 'Because I — unlike you, apparently — actually paid the author the courtesy of reading his work.'

Conor shrugged, nonchalantly.

'Mr Meade, whether you read the work or not is entirely up to you. Your failure to read set texts doesn't bother me one way or the other, because I, after all, will not be taking the exam based on them. And I certainly won't lose any sleep over your success or failure. However, when you are in this classroom, I expect you at least to have the good sense to admit your failure, rather than wasting everyone's time with your pathetic, infantile ramblings.'

Conor began to glower angrily. Mr Brady ignored him.

'Hear, hear,' shouted Gnasher from the back of the class. Much to Laura's surprise, a number of people applauded him.

'Ah, Mr Coyle,' said Mr Brady with a smile. 'I hope our little discourse didn't wake you from your slumbers too early.'

'Not at all,' replied Gnasher warmly. 'I'm wide awake and raring to go, as always.'

'Is that a fact, Mr Coyle? Then might I be so bold as to ask if you honoured Mr Ó Laighléis by reading his works?'

'Yes, sir. I did.'

'And your opinion?'

'They were really strong, and a couple of them — the one about the girl who died of AIDS, and the other one about the death of the bag lady — were very challenging emotionally. But what really impressed me was the way the author ended them — that dangling-ending trick.'

'Explain, please.'

'I can't remember how many stories it was used in, but .... Well, basically, in stories like the one about the gambler and the teacher, Ó Laighléis didn't give any definitive ending. He left the stories dangling. He ended them at a point where there were two or three different ways the character could go, and he left it up to us to decide which one we thought they'd take. So it's kind of interactive; we're not just readers, we're authors as well.'

'Very perceptive, Mr Coyle.' Mr Brady turned to Conor. 'Perhaps, Mr Meade, you should take notes on that and see how it was done.' He turned back to Gnasher. 'And can I expect that quality in your written answer?'

'No, sir, because I doubt if I'll do one.'

'Your prerogative entirely, Mr Coyle.'

'Yes, sir, I know.'

Laura heard Sarah, behind her, whisper, 'Dickhead.' Cass and Tina giggled on cue.

'Well, now then ....' said Mr Brady, looking around the room.

'Laura — Laura, it's me, Rosa. I need to talk. Can we talk?'

'Not yet. Give me a second.'

Laura rose to her feet. 'Please, sir, I need to go out.'

'Do you need anyone to go with you?'

'No, I'll be fine.'

'OK.'

She went down the corridor and into the girls' changing-room.

'I tried calling you last night, and so did Sanjid,' she said as she lay down on one of the benches in the changing-room.

'I know. I had to .... I couldn't answer.'

'Never mind,' said Laura, relieved to hear Rosa's voice again. 'When you get here, we can talk all night.'

'I won't be coming, Laura. Not now.'

'Why not?' asked Laura. 'You said you'd have your passport. I have the money — well, almost — and you just have to —'

'They raided Joseph's place last night, looking for drugs. They found my photos.'

'Oh, Christ!' exploded Laura, putting her face in her hands.

'That's what Freddy told me last night.'

'Well, can this Freddy help you get away?' Laura was shaking her legs nervously.

'Freddy?' She could hear the irony in Rosa's voice. 'Freddy's one of *them*, from Candelaria. We call him Freddy after Freddy in the *Nightmare* films, because he's our fucking nightmare. He enjoyed telling me about the photos last night, loved every second of it. He kept me here to play with.'

Laura felt a strange calm creep over her.

'Link with me, Rosa.'

'No!' snapped Rosa.

'Link!' said Laura firmly.

'No, Laura, please don't make me,' said Rosa, almost in tears.

'Goddammit, Rosa,' Laura ordered, 'I said link with me.'

Laura felt the pain between her eyes. She snapped

them closed. The blue light was so intense she felt as if
it was burning her. Then it eased.

She was in a small, dimly lit room.

'Where are we?'

'In a shack on the outskirts of the city.'

'Can you get out at all?'

'No way. The door's bolted and the window's
barred, look.'

As Rosa looked around the room, Laura saw that
the only furniture was a filthy mattress on the floor.
There was a half-empty liquor bottle beside it, and
three other empty bottles were strewn around the
room. The only other thing in the room was a full-
length mirror propped against a wall.

'Stand in front of the mirror. Let me see you.'

'No, Laura ....'

'Please, Rosa?'

'But why? What good will it do?'

'I don't know,' said Laura, hopelessly. 'I don't. I just
— I have to ask.'

Rosa walked over and stood in front of the mirror.

'Oh Jesus,' shrieked Laura. 'What has that fucking
bastard done to you?'

Rosa's right eye was swollen closed. Her nose was
twisted and bloody. Her lip was black and swollen.
There were bruises on her neck. Her blouse hung in
shredded rags, barely covering her shoulders. Laura
could see bite-marks and bruising on her breast, and
big round welts that looked like cigar burns on her
nipples and her stomach.

'The bastard, the fucking bastard,' Laura cried,
weeping. 'It's all my fault. I sent you to get the passport from Joseph. Rosa, I'm so sorry I did this to you.
Please forgive me.'

'I told you before, Laura,' said Rosa softly. 'I told

you: it was only a matter of time.'

'But I made them come. I did it,' Laura wept.

'Listen, Laura,' said Rosa. 'I was scared shitless for four years. I didn't give a damn about anything — I'd given up. But these last few days, I started to .... I had hope. You gave me that.'

Laura couldn't reply. She sobbed uncontrollably, but even through her tears she could still see the small, round, battered face looking back at her from the mirror.

'Laura,' said Rosa softly. 'I want to show you something.'

She pulled her skirt and her pants down below her hip, and angled the mirror so that Laura could see the butterfly crudely tattooed on her hip in Indian ink.

'Paulo did that,' she said. 'And I did one for him. The old Buddhist told us that when we die, we'll come back as something beautiful. I pray I'll be a butterfly.'

'But you can't just let them .... Tell me where you are — tell me what they're like — and I'll get someone to come and save you,' Laura cried.

'I can't. I ....' Rosa began. Then she stopped. 'OK, Laura,' she said calmly. 'I'm outside the city. There are two tall men with brown moustaches, driving a white Ford. They'll probably take me to Aterro do Flamengo Gardens — I heard Freddy say something about that.'

'I'll ring our government, and the police, and —'

'Laura. They won't be back for hours. Take your time. Stop crying and calm down, or you can't help me.'

'I will, I will,' promised Laura, controlling her tears.

'Good,' said Rosa calmly. 'Promise you'll wait a couple of hours before you do anything. Wait till you've calmed down.'

'I promise.'

'Swear on the Virgin.'

'I swear.'

'Good. I'll hear from you then. God bless. I've got to go now.'

As the voice faded, Laura heard a car screeching into the school playground.

She crossed to the wash-basins and plunged her head under the cold water. Then she dried herself on the towel hanging from the roller. She had to be calm; she'd promised Rosa. She had to be calm to help.

She sat down on the bench and crossed her legs into the lotus position, the way her mother had shown her. She let her chin fall on her chest and placed her hands, palms up, on her knees. She allowed her breath to become slow and even. Then, breathing deeply, she filled her body with the sound 'om', letting it rise slowly from her stomach to her mouth.

Slowly, as she repeated it, she felt her body and mind begin to relax.

chapter
19

'Aterro do Flamengo Gardens,' Laura repeated, as she crossed the fields leading out to the main road. 'Aterro do Flamengo Gardens.'

Gnasher had said that the best way to get money to Brazil was via the Franciscans. They were her best hope. If she could tell them what was happening, they could phone their missionaries in Brazil, and they could contact the local police, or go and save Rosa themselves.

Laura quickened her pace. She didn't feel she should waste any time. Rosa's words had given her some comfort and taken away her panic, but she still felt a great sense of urgency.

'Laura! Laura, wait up.'

Laura turned around. Conor was coming through the bushes. His shirt was half open, and there was grass on the knees of his trousers.

'Look, Conor, I don't have time to —'

'You disappeared at lunch-time, and I wanted to talk to you about the hash and —'

'Listen, Conor, I really don't have time for this. It can wait till —'

Conor grabbed her arm and spun her around. 'No, dammit. You're going to listen.'

'Conor, come on back and ....' a voice called from the bushes.

Laura spun around. Sarah was coming out of the bushes. Her school blouse was open to the waist. She was wearing the red bra with black lace edging.

'Oh, hi, Laura,' she said sweetly, draping herself around Conor. 'We were just ....'

Conor pushed her away roughly. 'Would you ever go and button yourself up, you prat.'

Sarah blushed.

'I swear, I didn't do —' Conor protested.

'Conor, I don't give a damn what you and Sarah do or don't do. I've got something more important going on.'

'Like what?' demanded Conor.

'Oh, fuck off. I don't have time for this crap.' Laura shook her arm free and pushed Conor away.

'I'll see you tonight, to explain,' he called, as Laura stormed off.

'That told 'em,' said a voice from nowhere. Laura spun around. She couldn't see anything but trees, and a few old wooden pallets here and there.

'That really told him.'

Two of the pallets leaning against an old oak moved slowly to one side. Inside, the tree was hollow; Gnasher, Kelz and a couple of the others were sitting there.

'Welcome to Aladdin's cave,' said Kelz.

Laura smiled. Inside they had a little carpet, and a few small wooden boxes for chairs.

'Listen, I can't stop. I've —'

'Yeah, we know you're in a rush,' said Gnasher.

'They didn't do anything, you know,' said Kelz. 'I mean Big-Mouth and Superbitch. We had a bird's-eye view from here. She undid her own blouse and —'

'Barbara, I honestly couldn't care less.'

'OK,' said Kelz. 'It's just that — I mean, we could never figure it out, but we thought you and him ....'

'Not a chance,' said Laura. 'Listen, I've got to go.'

She turned and walked quickly away. At the edge of the field, the path led to a small pedestrian path; Laura hurried onto it.

'She's dead,' screamed a little voice in her head. 'Laura, she's dead.'

'Sanjid, what are you —'

'She's dead,' screamed the little voice again. 'In that shed. They put the gun in her mouth and pulled the trigger. I was joined. I saw them do it .... She's dead. Laura, they killed Rosa. They blew her head off.'

Laura gagged for breath. Rosa had lied to her. The car she'd heard hadn't been in the schoolyard. It had been them. They'd come for Rosa, and she'd sent Laura away for her own protection. She'd known they wouldn't be taking her to Attero do Flamengo Gardens. She'd known that it would happen, not in a few hours, but within minutes. So she'd made Laura break the link.

Laura leaned against a wall. She felt as if her chest was going to burst.

'They tied her hands behind her back. They made her get down on her knees, and they murdered her,' screamed Sanjid. 'I saw them do it. I broke just as they squeezed the trigger. She's dead, Laura. Dead!'

Laura felt every muscle in her body tense. She screamed, a howl of anguish which carried with it every ounce of emotion she had.

'*No!*'

Then she was running. She could hear feet running behind her, Gnasher and Conor calling to her.

'Laura, what's wrong?'

'Laura!'

But she was running, faster than she had ever run before. Tears filled her eyes and spilled down her cheeks as she ran and ran and ran.

chapter
20

Laura stumbled through the door, exhausted. Her left hip was still throbbing. Instinctively, she put her hand down and rubbed it.

'Is that you, Lar?' her mother called from the kitchen.

'Yeah.'

'Are you OK?' asked Chris, emerging from the kitchen holding a cup of coffee. 'David Coyle called a while ago to see if you were home. He seemed concerned. He said something about you running off screaming.' She smiled as she said it, obviously relieved that Laura didn't look anything worse than tired.

'Oh, he's an awful worrier,' Laura lied, forcing a smile. 'I was going for a walk and I got harassed by some over-friendly gnats or something.' Lying was coming quite naturally to her now.

'Well, dinner's almost ready, and I've just made fresh coffee if you want some.'

'I need a shower first. I'll be down in a few minutes.'

'OK.'

Laura dragged herself upstairs and into her bedroom. She flopped down on the bed.

Her legs and hips were aching. She had no idea how long she'd been running, or where she'd run. She recalled vague, blurred snatches of places: the foot of the mountains, the old castle, the canal barges, the mills. But none of it made any sense. All she remembered was running, running and crying for a friend she'd never touched, a girl she'd never even seen in the flesh. Now she never would.

She must have crossed roads and raced through traffic, but she hadn't seen any. All she'd seen was a small, round face with big eyes, smiling at her. Funny: she'd never seen Rosa smile. She'd never seen her when her face and body weren't battered and bruised. She never would. But when she'd been running, it was that smiling face, young and alive, full of hope and promise, that had run with her.

'What a fucking disaster,' she sobbed softly, kicking off her runners.

The only thing she could recall with any clarity about the previous few hours was the pain, that and finding herself standing on the corner of Burgh Quay, looking across the Liffey at Liberty Hall. She had no memory of getting there; neither could she recall why she'd walked past Liberty Hall and up Gardiner Street towards that place. But as soon she'd seen the sign in the window above the camera shop, it had made sense. She hadn't been looking for it, but when she saw it she knew why she was there, why her run had ended at that place. Something in some part of her mind she didn't yet know about had brought her there, so she would remember Rosa for ever.

She reached under her pillow and grabbed her diary.

They murdered Rosa. They put a gun in her mouth and blew her head off. And it was my fault. If I hadn't made her get those papers ....

The world is full of fucking scum who murder poor little kids like Rosa and beat the hell out of kids like Sanjid.

I'll find some way to get him away from the carpet sheds, even if I have to walk to Mirzapur and do it myself.

Bastards! Lousy fucking bastards!

She threw her diary under her pillow, tugged off her sweatshirt, T-shirt and sports bra and pulled her dressing-gown around her. Carefully she slipped off her tracksuit bottoms and pants, taking care to avoid the plaster on her hip.

She went into the bathroom and turned on the shower. Hot water spurted out, splashing the tiles on the wall. Laura let her dressing-gown fall to the floor and stepped into the shower. The water was warm and soothing. Laura tilted her chin, letting the water mingle with the tears on her face.

She couldn't even remember the bus journey home. Sometimes the pain in her hip and some old drunk singing had brought her back, but most of the time she'd been crying and talking to the smiling face inside her head.

She picked up the soap and rubbed it all over herself. As she put it back on the shelf, she saw the small, hard-bristled shower-cleaning brush hanging beside it. She picked it up, pushed the bristles hard against her

shoulders, and dragged it roughly across her collar-
bones and onto her breast. It hurt, but she couldn't
stop herself. She wanted it to hurt, wanted it to scour
deep into her body, to wash away the pain of Rosa's
loss and the filthy degradation they'd inflicted on her.
She needed the hard bristles to tear at her skin, cleansing away the guilt of having brought that pain and
degradation on someone who had trusted her.

She dragged the brush across her stomach, towards
her thigh. The side of her hand touched the plaster on
her hip and she cried out in pain, dropping the brush.
She lowered herself to a sitting position on the floor of
the shower, curled her knees up to her chest, let her
head fall onto her knees and sobbed, heavy convulsive
sobs that made her whole body shake.

'Rosa, Rosa, I'm sorry. Forgive me. Please forgive me.'

She heard rapping on the door.

'Lar — Lar, are you still in there?' called her father,
chuckling. 'This isn't Parliament, you know. No all-
night sitting allowed in here.'

Laura shivered. The water pouring down on her
was freezing. She didn't remember it changing from
hot to cold.

She pulled herself up, turned off the shower, opened
the curtain and grabbed a towel.

'I'll be out in a minute, Dad.'

'It's OK. You've been in there so long I was just
checking that you hadn't slipped down the plug-hole
or anything.'

Laura wrapped a towel around her head and stepped
out onto the bath-mat.

'Laura, Laura,' sniffed a little voice inside her head.
'It's me, Sanjid.'

Sanjid! Laura couldn't even remember breaking the
connection with him earlier, but she must have.

'Sanjid,' she replied softly. 'How are you?'

'I feel like there's a big hole in my stomach,' he said. 'An empty place. A sadness, for my poor, sweet Rosa.' He sobbed softly.

Laura didn't reply.

'And I'm cold, and scared, and my back and my legs are sore from the beating Babu gave me.'

'Bastard!' said Laura angrily. 'Why did he beat you?'

'When I saw Rosa and the ... the ....' Sanjid choked, trying to finish the sentence. 'Then, when you were gone, I went crazy. I was yelling and shouting and tearing at the wool on the loom, slashing at it with my knife. And he ran at me and I tried to slash him too. When he grabbed me, I was scratching and kicking him. And I bit his hands and tried to run, but they grabbed me and dragged me back. Then they beat me, three of them, my master and two guards. They beat me with batons on my back and my legs and arms, till I passed out. And when I woke up I was in here, in the hole, under the floor.'

'Bastards,' screamed Laura, pushing the towel against her mouth. 'I'll get you out. I promise I will, Sanjid, I'll ....'

'Laura, I'm scared. I heard Patit's father is coming back with armed men. Babu Krishna is furious. He's beating everyone, and threatening to kill us all. And he will, I know he will. I've heard about other kids who tried to run away and were shot by guards. Laura, I'm scared and I miss my mother.'

'Sanjid ....'

'Let me see your family, Laura — your home, your mother,' he sobbed. 'If I'm going to die, I'd like to die knowing that I was part of a family again — even just for a little while, even if I can't touch them or feel them. Let me join with you. I won't be any trouble.'

'Sanjid, I don't know how ....'

'You just let it happen, Laura, just say it's all right and I'll do it. Please. I won't hurt. I won't be any trouble, I promise.'

'Then do it,' Laura replied softly. 'But don't be frightened. I swear I won't let them ....'

She stopped. She couldn't say it. She couldn't say the words 'I won't let you die'. She'd made that promise to Rosa.

She leaned over and cleaned the mist from the mirror of the bathroom cabinet as she waited to feel something that would let her know Sanjid had joined with her. Her shoulders were red and sore where she'd torn at herself with the brush. She stepped back so that she could see her breasts and stomach.

'I don't think I should. be seeing this,' giggled a sad little voice in her head.

'Jesus!' Laura grabbed the towel and covered herself, turning away from the mirror.

'I thought .... I didn't know — I ....' she stammered; and then she laughed, and Sanjid laughed with her.

chapter
21

Sanjid said so little that Laura found it easy to forget they were linked. There was none of the surprise or excitement she'd felt as Rosa had taken her around Rio. After a while she realised he didn't need to say anything; she could feel his happiness and satisfaction at being part of a family again. It was only at the end of the evening, as Laura began to get ready for bed, that he spoke.

'Laura, could you hug your parents and your sister and your brother good night? It's been so long since anyone hugged me. I'd like to feel it, just once more.'

Laura wanted to tell him to stop talking like that — to tell him that, somehow, she would find a way to make things OK for him. But she couldn't say it, because she didn't know if it was true. She wanted it to be true; she desperately, passionately wanted it to be true. But just because she wanted it, that didn't mean it would happen. So she said nothing.

She put her arms around her mother, hugged her tight and kissed her cheek. 'Night, Mom.'

Instinctively her mother hugged her back. 'What's that for?'

'Just for being you,' said Laura softly.

'And what about me just being me?' laughed her father. 'Don't I get one too?'

'Of course,' smiled Laura, and flung her arms around his waist. He locked his arms around her and grabbed her in a soft bear-hug.

'Hey! Don't break me!' she laughed.

Katie was sitting in the front room watching television. Laura bent down to her and gave her a hug and a kiss on the cheek.

Katie giggled with delight. 'Do that again,' she said. 'I still like cuddles sometimes, you know.'

Laura did it again.

'I think we'll make this a new family tradition,' she said, pushing herself up. She looked at Kev.

'Well, you can piss off if you think you're going to hug me, you mad prat,' he said.

'Who'd want to?' said Laura. She turned to Katie, smiled and wiggled her fingers. Katie nodded and stood up. They turned as if they were about to leave the room; then, on a nod from Katie, they turned and launched themselves at Kev. Laura lay across his chest, pinning his arms with her right arm and shoulder; with her other hand she began tickling him. Katie did the same. Kev kicked and wriggled, convulsed with laughter.

'Works every time,' chuckled Katie.

'No .... Gerroff .... Oh please ... please,' Kev screamed, helpless with laughter. 'Oh no ... stop ... stop, please ....'

He managed to twist and shake Laura off. Katie jumped back instantly.

'You bitches,' Kev laughed, red in the face. 'I hate you!' They knew he didn't mean a word of it, but they still raced from the room, with cushions flying after them. Laura ran upstairs, into her bedroom. Katie dashed into the kitchen and slammed the door behind her. They needn't have bothered. Kev fell back onto the sofa and carried on watching TV.

Laura could hear Katie giggling downstairs. She was aware of her own laughter, and she also heard the sound of Sanjid's gentle laughter inside her head.

'Thank you, Laura,' he said warmly. 'That's what I miss most of all — hugging and playing and laughing, with my family.'

It's so easy to take it all for granted, thought Laura, *the things that are so much a part of my everyday family life. I never even think about them.*

She undressed, facing away from the mirror. Taking care to avoid the sensitive spot on her hip, she pulled on her T-shirt and climbed into bed.

'Tell me about your family, Sanjid,' she said softly.

'I can't,' he replied sadly. 'I can't. When I first got here I thought about them all the time, every day, but that just made me want to cry. So I made myself stop thinking about them. Now, if I think about them, I don't know if what I'm remembering is really them or just my imagination.'

Laura could hear the soft, bitter sobbing.

'Sanjid,' she called softly, 'don't cry. Just be with me. We don't have to talk. Just be with me, and feel as if I'm holding you while we go to sleep. Let me be your family for now.'

She hugged her shoulders as if she were wrapping the little voice inside her head in a warm, loving embrace. The spot at the centre of her head became relaxed and peaceful. Without realising it, Laura began to sing the song her mother sang to them as she rocked them to sleep when they were scared or ill.

'Hush, little baby, don't say a word,
Mama's gonna buy you a mockingbird.
And if that mockingbird don't sing,
Mama's gonna buy you a diamond ring ....'

~

When she wakes, she can feel the dark, somewhere at her temples. It is only pencil-thin, but it is threatening.

She has never felt so scared and confused. Something awful is happening to her.

She tries to ignore it. She makes her way to school, telling herself it will be better once she is there.

And then, from somewhere outside herself, she hears a harsh, almost hysterical, voice. The voice is screeching, 'You're wrong!'

chapter
22

Laura Byrne, an observer to her own dying, floats higher. She sees the doctor take the diary from her mother's hands, watches as he reaches for a phone and presses numbers. He is saying words she cannot hear ....

Laura turns away. Something else is attracting her attention. It is a light, the most brilliant, comforting light she has ever seen. It is the soft rays of the sun mingling with the foam of a sea wave. It is the warm, gentle breeze of summer carrying the scent of apple blossom. It is the most welcoming, welcome feeling she has ever known.

The light draws her forward and she drifts calmly, peacefully, towards it.

And in the light something moves, something tiny and graceful. It floats towards her. Laura is not moving now. She is calm, waiting for the small, graceful thing that moves towards her.

Closer and closer it floats, growing as it comes. It is

so beautiful it must be a jewel. No, it is a flower with wings. No; it is a butterfly, small, delicate, perfect.

Silently, gracefully, it floats towards Laura. Then it is beyond her. She turns effortlessly. Where it leads she will follow.

Then she hears the sound. It is warm as a child's laughter, soft as the beating of a bird's wings, sweet as the first spring peach.

And the sound is a voice.

'It's not your time, Laura, my friend. Not yet.'

And Rosa's voice swells within Laura, pouring joy and love through every part of her.

'Not yet, my friend.'

Laura is back above the room where her body lies, where the doctors and nurses look at her.

'Not yet, Laura. I'll always be with you, but it's not yet your time to be with me.'

Laura floats above the table and the light. Then, instinctively as a diver turns his head to bring himself through the water back to the surface, she moves her shoulder and glides gently downwards.

chapter
23

Laura opened her eyes.

'Sanjid!'

She didn't know if she'd spoken it or thought it.

She turned onto her side. The hospital ward was dark. In the darkness she could make out the shapes of other patients, asleep in their beds.

A soft breathing behind her made her turn. Her mother was asleep in the chair beside her bed.

'Mom,' Laura called softly, not wanting to wake any of the others. 'Mom.'

Her mother opened her eyes, jumped out of the chair and leaned over to hug her.

'Oh, Lar!' she cried softly, her face pressed tight against Laura's as she held her. 'Oh, Lar, we thought we'd lost you that time .... We ....'

Her tears ran down Laura's cheeks and onto her neck.

'I'm sorry, Mom .... I should have ....' Laura's voice trailed off. She put her arms around her mother and buried her head in her hair. 'I'm sorry. So sorry.'

After a while Chris gently moved away, holding on to Laura's hand.

'I read your diary, Lar. You should have told us,' she said softly.

'I know,' said Laura. 'I know. I wanted to, but ....' Suddenly she remembered. 'Sanjid!' She said it urgently, anxiously.

'As far as I know,' her mother smiled, stroking Laura's cheek, 'the little boy is safe. You saved his life, Lar.'

Then she leaned forward and hugged her tightly again. 'But we could have lost you, Lar. Oh, Lar, you could have died ....'

Laura clung to her mother as they both sobbed softly, their tears saying more than words ever could.

One of the patients in the ward murmured something in her sleep. Chris gently moved away, wiping her eyes with the back of her hand.

Laura lay back on the bed. Suddenly, she felt completely drained.

'Lar, you're too tired to talk now,' said Chris, smiling. 'It's three in the morning. You should go back to sleep. I'll go now and come back in the morning.' She leaned over and kissed Laura on the forehead, then stood up. 'I just wanted to be here when you woke up. You've been through a lot.'

Laura nodded. 'Sorry,' she said again.

'The main thing is that you're all right. Get some sleep. I'll see you in the morning.'

Laura watched her mother walk out and have a quick word with the nurse at the duty desk. Then she closed her eyes and rolled over onto her side.

'Sanjid,' she called softly. 'It's me, Laura.'

There was no reply.

'Sanjid?'

She was too tired to call again. 'He must be asleep,' she mumbled, drifting away into her own sleep. 'He must be asleep.'

~

Laura woke to the sound of breakfast trolleys rumbling along the corridor. She sat up. She hadn't noticed it the first time she'd woken, but she had a drip connected to each arm. Her mouth was dry and the back of her throat felt raw. She wondered if that was how Sanjid felt. Then her mother's words came drifting back to her. 'You saved that little boy's life.'

'Sanjid,' she called softly; but something was different. It felt strange. It didn't feel the way it had when Rosa had blocked her. This was different ....

'Sanjid?'

Suddenly Laura realised she was just calling to herself. There was nothing there.

'Oh my God!' She put a hand over her mouth, afraid.

What if her mother had been lying? What if he was dead, like Rosa?

'Sanjid!' she screamed in her head. 'Sanjid!'

Nothing.

Laura closed her eyes tight and concentrated as hard as she could. 'Sanjid!' she screamed silently. 'Answer me, for God's sake. Sanjid!'

'Well, it looks like someone here has a severe case of constipation,' said a friendly voice.

Laura opened her eyes. Dr Heffernan was pulling the curtains around the bed. Laura glared at him angrily. She didn't need his interruption.

He saw the look.

'Ah! Trying to contact your pal ....' He took a bit of paper out of his pocket. '... Sanjid? Is that what you're at?'

Laura looked at him in silence.

'Well, with any luck,' smiled Dr Heffernan, 'he'll be doing what you've just been doing — sleeping. He's with SACCS now.'

'Who?'

'The South Asian Coalition on Child Servitude.'

'What?' Laura looked blank.

'Before we get into all of that, I need to talk to you about something else.'

He sat down in the chair beside Laura's bed. 'The thing is,' he said quietly, 'I'm not quite certain where to start.' He paused for a second. 'OK, let's try it like this.'

He coughed nervously, smiled and shook his head.

'Do you believe in luck?'

'Luck?'

'Yes. You know, good luck, bad luck, a lucky break — coincidence, I suppose you can call it.'

'Do we have to do this?' Laura asked, wondering anxiously about Sanjid.

'Yes, we do,' said Dr Heffernan, smiling. 'Now, do you believe in luck?'

'I suppose so. Why?'

'Because, young lady, you've just had the most amazing piece of luck ever. I wasn't even supposed to be on today.'

'And?'

'And it's your good luck that I was.' He laughed, rubbing his eyes. 'God, you've no idea how lucky you were. Anyway, when I saw you coming in I thought "asthma attack", and that was a fair enough assumption, given your history; but when I leaned over you I thought I could smell a hint of smoke, which didn't make sense. You hadn't been anywhere near a fire —'

'Sanjid!' Laura exclaimed.

Dr Heffernan held up his hand. 'In a sec,' he said.

'The next thing I know, your mother's pushing your diary at me — weird reading, to say the least. And that's where the luck comes in again. If anyone else in this hospital had read your diary and seen your admissions charts for the last couple of weeks, they'd have put two and two together and concluded that you were suffering from drug-induced delusions, and you'd have been hauled off to a psychiatric hospital — presuming, that is, that you survived.'

'And you?'

'Do you remember what I told you last time you were in, about me going off to Nepal and all that?'

Laura nodded, still uncertain where this was leading.

'Well, as part of my training for Nepal, I've been going to courses to familiarise myself with that part of the world, and that's where I heard about SACCS.'

'The South Asian ....'

'South Asian Coalition on Child Servitude. They're a charity working to eliminate child labour in Asia. I've seen videos of the work they do with child labourers in the glass industry, quarries, fireworks factories and ....' He paused and smiled. '... the carpet sheds. Now, the thing is, hardly anyone here's ever heard about the carpet slaves; and yet your diary entry describes the conditions so perfectly that I didn't see how you could be making it up.'

'So you believed me?'

'Well, let's put it this way. One the one hand, I have a patient who's been nowhere near a fire but is suffering from symptoms of smoke inhalation, and who claims to have some sort of link with a kid in a carpet factory. And on the other hand, I know that during some of SACCS's raids to free child slaves, things have got pretty rough, and people have been hurt.

'So I had to ask myself: could there be a link between

what was happening to you and what you'd written in your diary? And the simple answer was that I'd no idea. But you weren't responding to the normal treatments, and I didn't have any other ideas. So — it was nuts, I know, but what the hell — I made a huge leap of faith, rang Christian Aid and asked them to check if SACCS had just carried out any raids. And — thank God for e-mail and mobile phones — they contacted SACCS.'

'And?' asked Laura anxiously.

Dr Heffernan smiled.

'SACCS had raided a carpet shed following a complaint from some kid's father.'

'Patit Lal!' said Laura. 'His father said he'd come and get him.'

'Must be,' said Dr Heffernan. 'Anyway, during the raid there was a struggle, some small gas cookers got knocked over, and the place went up in flames. They got all the kids out, but everything happened so quickly that no one remembered your friend Sanjid. They were already heading for the local court, to get a letter of freedom for the kids, when they got the call from Christian Aid. Suddenly it was panic stations — everyone remembered he'd been put under the floor as a punishment. They raced back, breaking every speed limit, and managed to fight their way through the blaze and drag him out. He was more dead than alive, but at least he *was* alive.'

Laura put her head in her hands and cried. He was safe.

Dr Heffernan put his arm around her.

'Not only is he alive, but he's free. Soon he'll be back with his family again.'

Laura couldn't speak. The word 'free' danced around her mind, filling her with joy. Her whole body shook with tears of delight.

After a couple of seconds Dr Heffernan took his arm away and handed her a tissue.

'Now, I have a problem,' he said, still whispering. 'I can hardly put all that on your report, can I? I mean, who'd believe it? They'd probably have us both committed to a mental hospital.'

Laura smiled.

'Or, alternatively, they'll have you carted away somewhere to be tested for ESP, and you'll become some sort of celebrity guinea pig. I don't think you'd fancy that.'

Laura shook her head.

'The only people who really know what happened are you, your parents and me,' Dr Heffernan continued. 'Now, the thing is, you are an asthmatic, and a lot of the signs you were exhibiting would be there in a severe asthma attack. So, with your agreement, that's what I want to put on your chart: severe asthma attack. But if I do that, you'll have to swear never to mention this to anyone. If you did, I'd be in huge trouble.'

'That's fine by me,' said Laura. 'I swear. But I thought you guys altered charts all the time.'

'Only on *ER* or *Chicago Hope*,' he laughed, pulling back the curtains. 'Not in Saint Peter's.'

He started to leave, but then he turned and came back to Laura's bedside.

'I don't pretend to understand how all this happened, Laura,' he said quietly. 'But the outcome could have been serious, even fatal, for you. Speaking as a friend, you were nuts to let yourself get dragged into this sort of thing.'

chapter
24

Laura watched her parents walk past the nurses' station. She'd spent the morning alternating between looking forward to their visit and dreading it. She had no idea how they would react to what had happened. She'd tried to imagine herself in their situation, but she couldn't. Strange — she could share the thoughts and feelings of two kids thousands of miles away, but she couldn't imagine the thoughts of the two people closest to her.

Would they be angry? Scared? Annoyed with her for not telling them what was going on? Furious with themselves for not realising something was happening to her?

As Chris and Joe Byrne came into the ward, Laura felt a sudden pang of guilt. Why? It wasn't as if she'd taken drugs, or become pregnant. What did she have to feel guilty about?

As soon as she saw her parents' faces, she knew. They looked pained and anxious, and it was her fault.

For once her father didn't greet her with a big smile and a bear-hug.

'Are you OK, Lar?' he asked quietly, lowering himself into the chair beside her bed. Chris leaned over and gave Laura a kiss.

'I'm fine, Dad, fine.'

'That's good.'

He sat looking at the floor, without speaking. Laura had only seen him that quiet once before — the night his mother had died.

'Dad?'

He didn't look up.

'Dad ....'

'I'm sorry, Lar,' he said, wiping his eyes with his thumb and fingers. 'This whole thing's just knocked me sideways.'

He leaned over and took Laura's hand, holding it tightly in both of his.

'You should have told us,' he said softly. 'You should. That poor girl — the little guy — and you trying .... We'd have helped, Lar. We really would ....'

Laura watched him struggling to compose himself. 'I'm sorry, Dad,' she said. She felt tears in her own eyes. 'So sorry.'

Joe pulled her to him and held her tightly. 'You could have died, Lar. We could have lost you ....' Laura could feel his shoulders shaking as he tried to stop himself from crying.

'I'm sorry,' she sobbed. 'Honest, I'm really sorry.'

'You could ....'

He let it trail off. For a moment they moved beyond words. All they needed was the comfort of being close to one another.

When the moment passed, it was Chris who spoke first.

'You really should have told us, though, Lar,' she said gently. 'You didn't have to go through it alone.'

'I know. It was just ....'

'And what about next time, if there is one?' Chris continued. 'Maybe the sewer kids of Peru, or the child prostitutes in the Philippines, or some abused kid in Dublin. What then?'

Laura hadn't even thought about a next time.

'We nearly lost you once, and we don't want it to happen again,' said her father gently. 'So, Lar, promise us — please, promise — that if anything like this ever happens again, you'll tell us. We can't see inside your head.'

Laura nodded. 'I will.'

'Promise?'

'I promise.'

Her father smiled and relaxed. 'I'm happy with that.' He leaned forward and kissed her cheek.

Laura looked at her mother. 'And you, Mom? Are you OK with that?'

'I suppose so. I'm just wondering where you go from here. You won't just forget what you've been through, you know.'

'I know.'

'It'll take some time to come to terms with it.'

Laura nodded again.

'But what do you want to do about it? Is there something you can do to help kids like your friends Sanjid and Rosa?'

Laura shook her head. 'I've no idea.'

'Neither have I. But maybe we should think about it — not right now, but later.'

'I think Chris is right,' added Joe. 'We should think about that — later.'

He paused for a moment.

'So, what do you want us to bring when we come in tonight?' he said, deliberately changing the mood.

~

After her parents left, Laura drifted off to sleep. When she woke up there was a small parcel on her bed.

She opened it slowly. Inside was a T-shirt with the words 'Been there, done that, bought the T-shirt' printed on it. Pinned to the sleeve was a short note.

'If you need to talk, I know how to listen.

'Deco D.'

She'd found the secret admirer.

chapter
25

Laura looked at the photo propped against her art project. He was young, much younger than she'd expected. She'd thought he was about eight, maybe nine, but the letter from Mukti Ashram said he was six. Six years old, and he'd spent two of those years tied to a carpet loom.

During the two weeks she'd spent with her family in Donegal, just relaxing and doing nothing, she'd read some of the articles that Mrs Taylor's husband had sent her. The librarian had been right: it was unbelievable. There were fifteen million children in bonded labour in India; three hundred thousand of them were working in carpet sheds. SACCS had already freed thousands of children like Sanjid from debt slavery.

But he was so young!

'A boyfriend?'

Laura looked up. Declan Donnelly was standing beside her, looking at the photo and smiling.

'Thanks a million for the T-shirt,' said Laura. 'It was really sweet of you.'

Declan nodded, shyly.

It was Laura's first day of school in more than a month. She'd only come in for art, and this was the first chance she'd had to talk to Declan.

'His name is Sanjid,' said Laura, picking up the photo. 'He's six years old, and for two years he was a slave in the carpet sheds of Mirzapur ....'

Once she'd started, she couldn't stop. Declan was a good listener, and within minutes Laura had told him everything she knew about Sanjid, SACCS, and Candelaria.

'That sort of knowledge can really overwhelm you, can't it?' he said softly, when she'd finished.

'You've no idea how much,' Laura replied, tears starting to run down her cheeks.

Declan gently wiped the tears away with his thumb.

'The question is,' he replied, as the bell rang for the end of school, 'where do you go from here? Now that you have the knowledge, what do you do about it?'

Laura shrugged. 'I don't know. I can't just go on as if I'd never heard about it all. I have to do something. Maybe I can start a letter-writing campaign in school, demanding justice for the people murdered at Candelaria and protection for the witnesses. Maybe I could organise a fund-raiser for Mukti Ashram, or —'

'Mukti who?' Declan asked.

'Ashram,' said Laura. 'It's the place where SACCS brings freed child labourers for rehabilitation and training. Maybe we can do a fund-raiser for them, or sponsor a freed child, or —'

Declan smiled at her. 'It's not easy to decide, is it? But, hey — nothing worthwhile ever is.'

Laura looked back at the photo. She couldn't talk to

Sanjid in her head any more. The 'magic' had gone as suddenly as it had come; but it had served its purpose. Sanjid was safe, and that was what mattered.

'Listen, would you fancy going for a coffee?' asked Declan, almost shyly.

'Sure,' said Laura. 'I'd love to, but only if you promise to tell me about that famous missing year of yours.'

'It was only eight months, actually, but I'll tell you some of it. Deal?'

'Deal.'

'I'll just grab my bag.'

~

Declan looked at Sanjid's photo as he sipped his coffee.

'I've seen a lot of little kids like him,' he said. 'Boys and girls. Bhutanese refugees.'

'Where's Bhutan?' asked Laura.

Deco pulled a pen from his blazer pocket and sketched a rough map on a paper napkin.

'This is India, there's Nepal, and there's Bhutan,' he said, pointing to various squares. 'And here's where the refugee camps for the Bhutanese are.' He circled an area in southern Nepal. 'The people in the camps are Bhutanese Hindus, ethnic Nepalese, who're being "ethnically cleansed" — driven out of their homes and off their lands — by the Bhutanese Buddhist majority.'

Laura listen attentively as Deco explained what he called 'the mild ethnic cleansing' that had been going on for more than a decade. 'I've never heard anything about that,' she admitted.

'Don't worry, you're not alone; most people here haven't. I only found out about it last November, almost a year ago, when I picked up this picture book done by the refugee children. But after I saw the drawings and read their stories, I couldn't stop thinking about it. That's why I headed off to the camps last Christmas. I had to do something.'

He became so animated, as he spoke about the work in the refugee camps, that Laura didn't say a word.

'Anyway,' he said, when he'd finished, 'now you know the great secret of the missing months. You're the only one outside my family who does.'

'Thanks for telling me,' said Laura. 'I promise I won't tell anyone else.'

'I know.'

Deco looked at his watch and stood up. 'We'd better go. I'll just pay.'

Gnasher was right, thought Laura. *We do have more in common than either of us realised.*

As Deco waited at the counter, Laura looked out the window. Conor and Sarah were walking along the pavement, talking heatedly; Tina was beside them, with a little smile on her face. Cass was walking on the other side of the road, alone.

Laura looked at the photo again. Sanjid had his hand stretched out towards the camera, palm open. Resting in the palm was a delicate, brilliantly coloured butterfly.

Laura smiled and placed her hand on her hip. It didn't sting when she touched it, not like it had on the day of Rosa's death.

'Rosa,' she whispered. She ran her fingers gently over the place where she would carry Rosa with her forever, the place where the tattooist had placed the small, delicate tattoo of the butterfly. 'Rosa.'

author's note

Although Rosa and Sanjid are fictional characters, their stories are based on fact. Millions of children all over the world live and work in conditions like those described in this book. This note offers some basic facts relating to some of the issues raised in this book, and a list of useful sources for anyone wishing to learn more.

Candelaria

Those who died in Candelaria Square in 1993 were: Paulo Roberto de Oliveira, aged 11; Anderson Thome Pereira, aged 13; Marcel Candido de Jesus, aged 14; Valderino Miguel de Almeida, aged 14; 'Gambazinho', aged 17; 'Nongento', aged 17; Paulo José da Silva, aged 18; and Marco Antonio Alves da Silva, aged 20.

On 24 August 1998 a former policeman, Marcos Aurelio Dias Alcantara, aged 30, was found guilty of murder and attempted murder for his role in the Candelaria massacre and was sentenced to 204 years in jail. The sentence is largely symbolic; under Brazilian law, he cannot serve more than thirty years in jail for the slayings. Alcantara recanted a confession made in 1996 and pleaded not guilty to all charges. He refused to answer any questions during the two-day trial, exercising his right to remain silent. His attorney, Alberto Louvera, said Alcantara had been 'psychologically coerced into confessing' and would appeal. Alcantara showed no emotion when he heard the verdict and sentence, and kept his head bowed as he was led away.

Wagner dos Santos, who identified the policemen as the shooters, now lives in Switzerland for his protection. He was not present at the trial.

Street Kids

There are no accurate figures for the number of street kids worldwide, but the UNICEF estimate of 100 million is generally accepted. The majority of these are in developing countries: about 40 million live in Latin America, 25 to 30 million in Asia, and 10 million in Africa. The other 20 million are found on the streets of developed nations. Most are boys.

The Candelaria massacre is probably the best-known example of extrajudicial murder of street kids, but it is by no means unique. In November 1998, an informational website called Streetkid (see below) carried a report by Jared Kolter of Associated Press, describing the discovery of the remains of twenty-five children in Pereira, Colombia. Forensic experts estimated that the oldest victim was sixteen, and at least half of the victims were aged ten or younger. Prosecutors consider it possible that the children may have been killed by vigilantes as part of a 'social cleansing' campaign against suspected juvenile delinquents. Similar discoveries of child victims of 'social cleansing' are common in many countries in Central and South America.

Even when street children are not at risk from 'death squads' and other agents of extrajudicial execution, they are still at risk from disease, exploitation, random and planned acts of violence, sexual abuse and arbitrary arrest.

On Tuesday, 2 February 1999, National Civil Police in Guatemala City detained eight girls and fourteen boys who were sleeping in an abandoned building. They were all under the age of eighteen. A judge ordered all of the youths detained, accusing them of 'public scandal'. Under the current Guatemalan Minors' Code, the children cannot have a lawyer to represent them — even though this is a clear violation of the UN Convention on the Rights of the Child, and of the Guatemalan Constitution.

At the time of writing, the release of the twenty-two children has become the focus of an international campaign, with Amnesty International and Casa Alianza calling on people to write to the Guatemalan government, demanding their release and calling for amendments to the laws governing child detention.

Children in Bonded Labour

Bonded labour occurs in parts of Africa, Asia and Latin America. As it is an illegal practice in all the countries in which it exists, there are no accurate figures for the number of children bound in debt servitude. UNICEF estimates that, of 200 million child workers worldwide, 150 million work in the five countries that form the Indian subcontinent: India, Bangladesh, Pakistan, Nepal and Sri Lanka. 25 million are bonded labourers. 15 million of these are in India.

Child bonded labourers are found in more than three hundred occupations and industries. These range from agriculture to domestic service, from garment manufacturing to the production of fireworks and matches, from brassware to carpet-weaving. Many, though not all, of these industries manufacture products destined for the West.

The South Asian Coalition on Child Servitude (SACCS)

SACCS is an umbrella organisation for four hundred child rights groups. SACCS's goal is 'total elimination of child labour from the South Asian region, ensuring free and compulsory universal elementary education for all children and, above all, restoring their precious childhood'.

Since its inception in 1989, SACCS has pursued a two-pronged strategy of direct action — freeing children from bonded labour, through raids such as the one described in *Is Anybody Listening?* — and indirect action, including marches and rallies, aimed at heightening awareness of child labour.

One child freed as a result of intervention by one of the organisations affiliated to SACCS was the young Pakistani boy Iqbal Masih. Sold into slavery at the age of four as a result of a six-hundred-rupee (approximately £8) loan taken out by his parents, Iqbal escaped six years later with the help of the Bonded Labour Liberation Front. For much of the next two years, he travelled the world as a spokesman for BLLF, exposing the scandal of child labour. In those two years, his words and actions helped to free three thousand other bonded child labourers.

Iqbal was shot dead on Easter Sunday, 16 April 1995, aged 12. There is a widely held belief that he was murdered by the members of the carpet-weaving industry.

Mukti Ashram

Mukti Ashram (House of Freedom) was opened by SACCS in 1991. The ashram, which is in Delhi, India, aims to help children who have been freed from bonded labour to overcome the traumatic effects of their bondage. It provides the children with basic education and vocational training and educates them about their rights and obligations. All expenses are borne by the ashram.

The ashram can accommodate seventy children. To date, it has trained two thousand children in different vocations.

One of these children was seventeen-year-old Nageshwar Rissideo, whose name was borrowed for one of the fictional characters in this book. Nageshwar worked in the carpet sheds of Uttar Pradesh for seven years before his rescue in 1995. When he arrived at Mukti Ashram, he was so shell-shocked that he was unable to utter a word about his experiences. Despite public outcry at the loom owners' treatment of Nageshwar — their brutalities included branding him with red-hot rods, marking him for life — the police officials took no action against them.

After comprehensive medical treatment and special care and attention from the ashram's staff, Nageshwar was able to return to his home. He now teaches carpentry to other children, and he is busy sensitising the village people to the ills of child labour. His ambition is to become a social worker; when asked why, he replies, 'To help other children in bondage.'

A play about his life, *Nageshwar's Story*, written and performed by Telltale Theatre Company, Cork, will begin touring Ireland at Easter 1999.

A percentage of the royalties from *Is Anybody Listening?* will be contributed to Mukti Ashram.

To Find Out More

Most major overseas aid organisations are involved in working to combat bonded labour. Five websites which offer links to all major organisations are:

ILO:

http//www.ilo.org

UNICEF:

http://www.unicef.org/

Anti-Slavery International:

http://www.tcol.co.uk/comorg/assi.htm

Global March Against Child Servitude:

http://www.globalmarch.org/

SACCS:

http://www.globalmarch.org/saccs/saccs.htm

All these organisations offer a number of excellent publications which explain the situation in further detail. They can also provide information about street kids.

Additional websites providing information on street kids and related issues include:

Streetkid:

> www.jbu.edu/business/sk.html

Casa Alianza:

> media@casa-alianza.org>

Both these sites have extensive links to similar organisations.

Two organisations in Ireland whose work involves the issues raised in *Is Anybody Listening?* are:

Trocaire:

> http://www.trocaire.org

Christian Aid:

> www.christian-aid.org.uk

Those wishing to do something more directly can show their solidarity with the children in Mukti Ashram and other child workers by sending letters, postcards, drawings or photos to the young people at the ashram.

Mukti Ashram can be contacted at:

> Mukti Ashram
> near Ibrahimpur
> Delhi 110036
> India

Mark all correspondence 'For Suman', and mention that you are writing as a result of her letter to Michael Begg of Christian Aid (Ireland).

Mukti Ashram can also be contacted by e-mail at:

> yatra@del2.vsnl.net.in

Larry O'Loughlin
Dublin
March 1999

New from Wolfhound Press!

Silent Stones

**the eagerly awaited new novel
from award-winning author**

Mark O'Sullivan

On the farm of Cloghercree stands an ancient circle of stones ....

Mayfly is there because her New-Age-traveller parents believe
the standing stones will miraculously cure her dying mother.
Robby is there because, trapped between his embittered
great-uncle and the shadow of his dead IRA father,
he can't escape.

But then Cloghercree is invaded by the ruthless terrorist
Razor McCabe, on the run from the police.
And as the shadows of the past begin to close in on them,
Robby and Mayfly know their time together is running out ....

By turns gripping, thought-provoking and deeply moving,
Silent Stones is the story of two teenagers forced to come to
terms with their own and their families' pasts.

ISBN 0-86327-722-5

Angels Without Wings

Mark O'Sullivan

Siegfried, Greta, Anna and Dieter are the Lingen Gang.
Their creator is Axel Hoffen, a popular adventure-story writer.
But it's 1934 in Berlin, and the Nazis want to control the
world — including the world of books. There is no place in
that world for Jewish Anna or one-armed Dieter.

Axel has a choice: write a new book, twisting the Gang to fit
Nazi ideals, or face torture and even death.

Then, like angels without wings,
Siegfried and Greta, Anna and Dieter step out of the book
to face the Nazis and the real world.

Can they put a stop to the evil Lingen Gang book?

Can they save Axel from the merciless SS?

Can they save themselves from being drawn back
into the fantasy world of Leiningen for all eternity?

ISBN 0-86327-591-5

White Lies

Mark O'Sullivan

For Nance, it begins with the photo she finds in her adoptive
mother's room — a photo of herself as a black baby,
with the parents she has never known.

For OD, it begins with his father's decision to buy a trumpet
— and with Mick Moran's strange visit
to the Town Park building site where OD works.

Both of them need to know the truth before their lives —
and their relationship — can go on.

But as their search continues,
they discover that everybody has secrets —
and that the truth is never as simple as it seems.

A White Raven Book

ISBN 0-86327-592-3

All books available from:
WOLFHOUND PRESS
68 Mountjoy Square
Dublin 1
Tel: (+353 1) 874-0354   Fax: (+353 1) 872-0207